The Astral Marten

Written By
Melinda Pearce

The Astral Marten

Melinda Pearce

Contents

Contents (cont.)

Introduction

This story began as an astral travel into another dimension, which took place in the year 2011. This amazing experience was not only followed a discernible storyline, but, because the experience was not limited by this physical realm, the traveler was able to know the thoughts, feelings, and motivations of each of the characters. As a result, the portions of the story that are described in the first chapter are told from the points of view of different characters, from which they describe their roles in the story and their points of view and experiences. Sam (Samantha) is the daughter of the car's inventor, Jackson Pearce, and is also the niece of the used car lot owner, Charles Pearce. Charles is Jackson's brother, is the owner of the used car lot, and is the person who rents out the Astral Marten. Lady Jamis is a fairly well-off, married woman, who is mysteriously led to the car lot, because she "absolutely must drive that car." After the first chapter, with a few exceptions, the experiences that people have with the car are described from the narrator's point of view. This is how it unfolded to me, during my astral travel, while my powerful mind entered into another dimension of reality.

The Astral Marten car really does exist, in a realm – in a dimension – with great knowledge and power, which could be described as the most superior realm of all realities. The travel experience clearly took place in another time and place from normal reality, but I, the traveler, am not at all certain where that place is. Knowledge, as recorded through experience, is known through the traveler's mind, and her body's terrestrial cells recorded details of the story, accurately, during the entire travel, even as multiple events unfolded. Her spirit-like energy floated, flew, and moved, while her physical body remained in this limited environment of Earth. The traveler remembered the story vividly, as it was presented to her, including every detail. When she awoke from this travel, she immediately felt a strong need to write down the details, as she recalled them, so that the whole experience may be remembered in the future. Now wide awake, she sat up in the bed and pondered on every single detail without delay; the scenes flowed out of her and onto the paper, as she wrote in detail of the experiences and events. The information was crystal clear and was to become a fascinating adventure that she would not forget. She knew it all had taken place for a specific reason.

She knew she would write a book on this experience, and as time progressed, it became evident to her, that all she had discovered, in all of her many astral travels, would need to be shared in numerous types of reading materials, so as to share specific spiritual information that she had known before this earthly life, but which had become lost in previous cycles of life. The traveler realized that there were several different audiences who may be interested, and that her experiences would pour into their imaginations, planting into their minds a message of a powerful knowledge that would invoke the powers of their minds to open up, so that they could be used productively.

May you enjoy this tale of The Astral Marten, Car of the Future!

Chapter 1

A Mysterious Lady Seeks the Astral Martin

Sam begins telling the story:

Here is how it all started, many years ago, beginning with the mysterious lady, who arrived like clockwork every three months to rent my late father's unique car. This car happened to be the coolest and only car in town with its unique design – especially, its metallic flakes of gold in the color, which depicted a vision of swirls of multiple Universes in a repeated motif, but subtly in the paint on the body, so you had to be up close to see it, as well as a unique, black, convertible top, with hundreds of woven antennas within the canvas. This car was not like any other vehicle ever created and was a very unusual car with mysterious capabilities. It operated strictly on ambient energy alone and did not require fuel to be powered. All who sat in this vehicle could experience that it harbored its own powerful environment. This unique environment created enrichment in each person who sat in the car, which would aid them to evolve to a more powerful and joyful reality, one that created a new existence and a new outlook in their current life.

It was early on a Monday morning, on December 7, 1970, approximately at 9:00 a.m. A lovely lady came to my uncle's car lot to inquire about the gold-colored car that was parked among the other cars that were listed for sale.

My Uncle Charles owned and operated a used car lot, which was on a corner at a busy intersection, in a very small town near Roswell, New Mexico. My uncle placed the asking price only on the front windshields of his cars, and then parked them so that the rear of each vehicle faced the busiest side street of his corner lot. He did this to prompt any prospective buyer to physically enter his lot, in order to see the asking prices on the windshields of his vehicles. This was a great marketing tool, to get buyers onto the lot, and it worked very well, too!

This lady, whose name was Jamis, and who was young and quite attractive, discovered to her surprise that the car she was inquiring about was not at all for sale, but rather, for rent only! She placed her index finger onto her lips, as she was confused by this discovery, and asked my uncle why the car was only for rent, while all the other vehicles were for sale?

My uncle, Charles, explained, "My brother, Jackson, designed, created, and built the car, by hand, twenty years ago, and it was a sentimental family heirloom to the entire family." Uncle Charles stated it was available for rent, because he thought it would be nice for other people to experience his brother's futuristic car. He also added, "Before my brother died, it was his profession to create futuristic cars. Jackson mastered the Science of creating this vehicle, so that it strictly operated from energy created by the elements of this planet, by utilizing energy from the environment, a discovery of Mr. Nicola Tesla in the late eighteen-hundreds." Uncle Charles further explained to Jamis about my father's passion and love for designing and creating cars, and how he spent most all of his time drawing futuristic cars, when he was not researching other properties of Science and helping to plow and tend the fields of the family farm, until he passed away fifteen years ago.

From that time, the car had been stored in Dad's workshop, covered, until six months ago, when I suggested to my uncle, and convinced him, to begin renting it to folks as a fun experience. I believed my dad would have been pleased that everyone could experience this aerodynamic car, that he designed and was so proud of creating. My uncle agreed, and he placed the Marten on his car lot, for rent.

As Sam briefly stepped away to take a phone call,

Charles continues the story:

I thought back to the day I witnessed my brother sitting in it. He had such a connection to this car. When my niece suggested renting the car to the public, it was as if my brother was present, though I knew that was impossible, because he had been dead for fifteen years.

I turned in for bed that particular evening, and my last thought, before I closed my eyes, was Sam and my brother, Jackson, and his beautiful, sleekly-designed, gold car, with a black, convertible top and white, leather interior. I drifted into sleep, and by the next morning, I decided that my niece, Sam, was correct, and so we have been renting it out for twenty-four-hour periods at a time for the past six months. Luckily, we have not had to do any repairs at all. That's a good thing, too, because I have no idea how to repair this car, if it did need repair. I have searched through Jackson's workshop, looking for the designs or even for the car's schematic of its mechanics, but I wasn't able to find anything describing the inner workings of this car. Luckily, it has always been returned in tip-top shape.

Without a reasonable doubt, my brother was a brilliant scientist, and he loved thinking, designing, and creating cars in his spare time. He would create prototypes, people would see his prototypes, and they just had to have a replica. But, the Astral Marten is in a class of its own, and the only one ever created by my brother. He left no details of how he engineered the car. No notes or blueprints. This car holds all my brother's secrets within its sleek design. It's a bad, furious, muscle car, with stealth precision, and it glides ever so easily down the long, distant roads around here. The front headlamps are skinny, pinstripe lights that extend over the entire grill and wrap slightly around each fender. No car has ever been designed as this car has been. Even today, I have no idea where my brother came up with such an out-of-this-world design.

The natural-looking, slightly smoky tint on the windows keeps the white interior in a cool climate. It is the strangest thing. It can be 100 degrees outside, and it never fails to remain a cool 70 degrees temperature inside the car. The convertible top has a massive amount of wired antennas woven into the canvas, for great reception, even to reach far distant radio stations – a good trick, since we are geographically located in a rural and desolate area of New Mexico. The car has such an energy about it, and it is undeniable how it has the ability to level out the energy of each person who sits in it. If they may have had a bad experience or a bad day, this car has the capability to help them feel empowered, like a free-spirited human. The energy is invitingly intense, but in a calm sort of way – the car has that positive effect on all who sit in it. The car was built out of my brother's love for it. For all who have driven this car, it has provided them with an absolutely remarkable and unforgettable experience.

Before Sam walked away to take a phone call, Jamis held on to every word my niece said, describing this car. Jamis was intrigued by every detail of the entire story of the history of the car and the man responsible for creating it. She most certainly was drawn to the car by the it's unique design.

*As Sam returned from her phone call, **the lady, Jamis, responded by conveying her experience, first speaking to Sam and Charles, and then narrating the story from her point of view:***

I must confess to you both. My husband and I had a late luncheon yesterday. On Sunday, after church, we were on our way home, when we were caught at the red light, at the corner of Tesla and Westinghouse. We were fifth in the line of traffic, and while we were waiting for the light to change, I looked over my husband's shoulder and noticed the used car lot on the left corner. I spotted the gold car and asked my husband, as a joke, "Will you buy me that gold car?" We could only see it from the rear side, and we could not see the asking price, but he immediately replied with, "We can't afford that car." Originally, I was only joking, but as we returned home, I could not get that car out of my mind! My attraction to this car was unbelievable, and the next morning could not come soon enough. I had return to the car lot to inquire about it and see the car up close. I drove here, first thing this morning, to just see it, so I could quench my desire of knowing the price, so I could get this car out of my mind. And now, I find that there is no price on the windshield, and it is for rent only, and *that*, for a twenty-four-hour period only! I cannot emphasize how disappointed I am!

While all the other vehicles are for sale, I am mesmerized only by this car – and, oh my, is it more than I ever imagined, up close! I could not believe how this car had such an enormous effect on my energy, while my husband and I were waiting for the traffic light to change! It was as though it was serenading me! As much love as I have for my husband, he does not have the effect on me that this car seems to have.

It is as though it is signaling me to "rent it now!" The style alone is not like any other vehicle on the road, nor any car I have ever seen before, in my entire life. I am married to a successful businessman and entrepreneur, and we have traveled the world, so I have seen a lot of cars.

[I found myself desiring to drive this car, and then I found myself trying to convince Charles of a ridiculous idea to rent the car to me for three days.]

Charles replied, "I don't know if I can do that. The car has not been out of our sight for that long of a period before."

I was determined to have this car for three days out of the present week! I continued to explain that the car seems to be making me feel I must rent it for that amount of time.

I told Charles, "I just have to have it, for just three days, and I promise I will return it right back to you on the morning of the fourth day! I promise, and I give my word faithfully!"

Finally, Charles gave in to my request, but he wanted to check with Sam, first. After all, it was her father who had designed and created the car, and the car would someday be passed down to her. Charles asked Sam to step a short distance away, so he could ask her privately. I could hear Sam agreeing to my request, whispering to her uncle, "She has some type of connection to the car! No one has ever behaved as she did, moments ago." They both agreed to allow it to be rented for three days.

When they returned to where they left me standing, Charles said he acknowledged how important it seemed to be to me, "to this very beautiful lady with such class and wit about her." I filled out the necessary paperwork, with my home address, driver's license, and proof of insurance. I paid the rental fee – in full – and drove the car off the lot, leaving my car behind.

The energy this car signaled out was amazing! I could feel the vibration of excitement it was signaling to me! This vehicle was truly unique in character, and it glided on the road, with no hesitation at all. Strangely enough, it seemed as though it were alive in some way. I enjoyed every turn and every stop! I noticed onlookers staring at me, as people turned their heads to watch the car, and to take in its beauty and elegance, until we were no longer in sight. I could not believe how this car made me feel – as though I am very powerful, in some way, and in complete control of my mind and spirit!

I felt that I was so free in my mind, that I could think and imagine all I desired and to experience each detail of every desire. By doing so, I did not realize that I was improving my reality, by the positive thoughts I was thinking. I drove the car down long country roads all day, and out of habit, I kept checking the gas gauge, that wasn't there, since the car runs on ambient energy. Time seemed to have flown, and, several hours later, I suddenly realized I needed to head home to prepare dinner for my husband! Upon my return home, I discovered that my husband, John, had finished his day early, and was waiting for me. He had also just arrived, moments before I did. When he saw I had the car, his face turned a pale white, and his jaw dropped. By the look on his face, he immediately thought I had purchased the car, after he had just said, the day before, that we could not afford to buy the car.

Before he could say a word, I quickly reassured him that I had only rented it, and explained the whole story to him. Even he was amazed that it was available only for rent, besides noticing the obvious beauty of the car. After he inspected it, he agreed with the lot owner, Charles, who made it perfectly clear he could never part with the car by selling it. I shared my special terms of renting the car (a special permission, three days' rental), and requested that he not share my special deal with anyone, in case they should demand the same terms. John agreed, noting the sense it made.

I then suddenly announced, with excitement, that I wanted to go visit my best girlfriends, Crista, Michelle, and Tiffany, in the next town over, which was less than two hours' drive away – that night. I planned to spend a couple of days away and wanted my girlfriends to take a long ride with the top down.

After dinner, I packed my overnight bag, kissed my husband, and said, "My love, I will see you in a couple of days."

In only a few minutes, I was on my way, in the futuristic car that was the coolest car around. I traveled for almost an hour down the long, country roads, driving toward my girlfriends in the next township, when I suddenly felt I needed to relieve myself. However, there was no place around that stretch of highway, no businesses or homes along this long winding road, at which I could stop and use the restroom – or, so I thought. In my next thought, I noticed, off to the right and in the distance, an old, abandoned, wood-framed house that had a long, dirt driveway leading to it. What was bizarre was, I had never noticed this house before, despite numerous trips I had taken to see my friends, while driving down this very same country road. I knew this road very well – and that house wasn't there, before.

Nevertheless, I had the thought, judging from the house's vintage appearance, that it may possibly have an outhouse, which may be still standing and also able to support my weight. So, I pulled the car behind the house and found that there was no outhouse in sight. Thinking there may be an inside restroom, I then walked briskly around to the front porch. The windows were boarded up, but the front door was usable – and unlocked – so, I went inside.

The craftsmanship of the house was amazing! All real wood, with unique designs carved into the wood. It felt like I was in another world. Oddly enough, instead of seeking out where the bathroom was located, I became sidetracked by the feeling that I had been there before. But, that was impossible, since I had never noticed the old house, before. Then I realized that I no longer needed to use the restroom, and walked straight past the bathroom and into the back bedroom, to the far left back of the room! I was drawn to investigate that corner of the room, completely forgetting why I had turned off into the long driveway, in the first place.

In the corner of the room, I knelt down onto the hardwood floor, and lifted several, short, hardwood planks. It was as though my hands knew which planks to lift! Under the planks were numerous letters and pictures. I put my glasses on and found that my vision was perfect, so I removed the glasses and placed them beside me on the floor. I then began to read all of the documents and carefully study the pictures. They had been hidden there, in the floor, by another person, but who could have put all these letters and pictures there? What did it mean, and how did I know to look under the loose boards?

I read and studied each sheet of paper, carefully. I had been reading for hours, before I placed all the documents and pictures back where I found them. As I placed each item back, one at a time, I carefully glanced over them, again. My thoughts were full of knowledge and understanding of numerous things, on numerous levels, that I had never considered nor imagined to be real, much less to be important. I felt mentally exhausted, from absorbing all that I had read, and before I knew it, I fell asleep, right there on the floor.

I went into a realm I had never experienced, before. It was so pure and lavish! The beings that were there were so intelligent. They seemed to want to praise me, and they were very happy to see me. I had never felt so much love, before, as I did in that moment! I awakened, and it was dark! It must have been a dream I experienced – I thought, clearly a place like that is not a place knowable to man. I had a feeling that I needed to return home that night, without delay. I didn't realize, until I arrived at home, that I had slept for two days, and it was nighttime of the third day – it was already time to return the car the next morning!

Upon leaving the house and arriving home, I made another startling discovery. Even though the windows were boarded up from the outside, looking in, this was certainly not the case for looking out of the windows from the inside. Through the windows, I viewed meadows of beautiful flowers of brilliant colors and recall hearing the harmony of birds chirping and singing. I knew, at that very moment, that everything I discovered would have to be kept a tight secret, within my mind. I honestly did not want to leave the old frame house. It was the most beautiful home I had ever seen, and, even though magical things happened in the house, I was not afraid at all. It was as if I was connected to it from another time and place, that I could not fully remember.

When I finally returned home, I discovered it was late Wednesday evening – the third day! I had spent Monday cruising in the car all day, Monday night

22

reading documents located in the floor, and Tuesday and Wednesday in an unconscious state, apparently visiting that other place, where there were beings who were so friendly and loving to me. I needed to return the car back to Charles on Thursday morning. My husband, John, was happy to see me, asked me how my trip went, and "How did the girls like the car?" I replied that I had a very enlightening experience. I was not able to divulge the loss of time, nor what I learned. I had a lot to consider. I had apparently gone into some kind of deep dream-like state of existence or meditation, while I thought I was reading those papers. It all seemed so real, when I was there, but now that I was back at my home, it seemed like a wild dream.

I told him again, "It was enlightening! And it was great! I had a blast!" I didn't tell him that I never made it to see my girlfriends. I was certain that no one would understand what had happened to me, while I was in that house, and it was up to me to carry on, as though nothing unusual had happened, because I could not clearly recall the events that transpired, anyway, although I learned amazing things, while I was reading the notes. Upon returning home, my memories of what I read became vague.

The next morning, I drove to the car lot and returned the car to Charles and Sam. I had to sign a form, upon returning the car, and it was at that moment that I realized that I had mistakenly left my reading glasses in that old abandoned house! I did not make a fuss about it. I just signed the form, as best as I possibly could, considering I only used the glasses for reading. Charles asked me how my trip turned out, and did my friends like the car? I replied to Charles that the trip was more than I could have ever imagined it to be, and then told him how I absolutely love the car, and that the night sky was quite enjoyable with the top down. After saying that, I paused, since I did not drive the car at night with the top down. I did not recant what I said, but, I just could not believe I uttered those words.

Before I left the car lot, that same morning, I simply had to reserve the Marten for three more days, every three months, beginning on the tenth day of every third month in a calendar quarter. I didn't know why I needed to reserve it in such a pattern, but I explained that it would be every three months, because my husband was so conservative with our money, and it would be a gift to me, four times a year.

Charles replied that, because he thought I was a genuine, likeable person, and that he could feel my calm energy, he trusted me completely, so, he agreed to rent the car to me every three months. He would continue to rent it to other people for twenty-four hours only, but would rent it to me for three days at a time. He asked me to not tell my friends of our agreement, because they could not rent it under the same terms that he permitted me to. I agreed, and promised to keep our agreement a secret, except for John, my husband, because I had already told him, and because he had to know, anyway, because I would be away with the car for three days at a time. After securing the agreement for the quarterly rental, I thanked Charles, wished his day to be a great one, and left behind the beautiful Astral Marten car.

Now back in my own car, I drove to return to the old house, to retrieve my reading glasses. I fully remembered placing them on the bedroom floor, when I began reading all those documents. But, something was not right! I drove up and down the main road, for hours, at least a half a dozen times, looking for that house, yet it was nowhere to be found! I began to think I was going senile, that I must have imagined all that I did, and had simply forgotten where I placed my glasses, but I knew deep inside that it was not my imagination, and that I knew exactly where I left my glasses. Not finding that house was upsetting to me, yet there had to be a reasonable explanation as to why I could not find the house. I felt exhausted from driving such long distances for nothing, and was ready to return home. Upon arriving home, I decided to rest a while, and took a nap. During my nap, I was able to remember all of what had happened at the abandoned house. I also knew I would see that house again in three months. It was also easy to replace my reading glasses with another pair, so I would not be without them.

Chapter 2

The Astral Marten Performs a Miracle

Charles would not see Jamis for the next three months. During the intervening months, numerous people would reserve the car and rent it. Charles continued to rent the car to local college kids on holiday, business people, government officials, and celebrities. The car grew to have quite a reputation, that one may have strange experiences, while the car is in one's care. Special events did not always happen with every rental, but when they did, it left a lasting impression on the individuals. Here is one of several stories with an unexplained occurrence.

Early in January 1971, two young, college-aged couples, Robert, Brandon, and their girlfriends, Joan and Alisha, rented the Astral Marten for a double date. They had planned to have a romantic dinner, followed by seeing a movie at a theater. The couples had earlier dined at a fabulous restaurant in town, known as "The Chancellor is Dining." While on their way to the theater, on a long, winding road, an oncoming semi-tractor trailer suddenly swerved into the lane of the Astral Marten. Robert was driving, and he quickly swerved to avoid being hit head-on. As he swerved, the car's wheels made contact with the gravel on the shoulder of the road, causing the Marten to spin out of control and head toward the steep rocky cliff. The car was literally off the

27

ground and was airborne, as it left the cliff's edge, spinning clockwise. The young people were all screaming, knowing they were most likely about to perish by plummeting down to the bottom of the cliff, especially with the convertible top down, when all of a sudden something bizarre happened. The car began to slow in mid-air, as the engine roared at a high velocity on its own, which generated pressured airflow from the exhaust pipes, that then caused the car to have propulsion to return the vehicle back to solid ground. The car's wheels quickly made contact with the ground, forcing the car to spin back onto the road.

Even with its known prestige and sport suspension capabilities, the car shocked the couples. Even the truck driver, who had quickly passed the spot where he would have hit the Astral Marten, and who forcefully applied his brakes, was shocked to witness the car returning back to solid ground, as he viewed through his side view mirror. It all seemed to have happened in slow motion, and the truck driver did not allow himself to believe what he had just seen. He was so upset, that he did not focus on what he had just witnessed, and chose to believe his eyes were playing tricks on him. Instead, he was dreadfully concerned about nearly crushing the car with four people inside, and he was sincerely regretful for veering into their lane. He asked the young people if he could do anything to get them home safely. The college kids were in shock, but were glad to be alive. They declined his offer and decided to end their evening, without seeing the movie. After dropping the young ladies back home safely, Robert and Brandon, who were roommates, drove directly home, and planned to return the car the very next morning.

On their way to the car lot, Robert and Brandon could barely wait to tell Charles what had happened to them and to explain to him how the car was able to take control and redirect back to the ground. They arrived at the lot, and Charles greeted them, but before he could ask them, "How did everything go," they explained what happened the evening before, and that they should be dead right now! They explained the entire event with great excitement, including how they had a miraculous recovery with this car!

Charles raised an eyebrow, but he was not surprised at all. He had heard others tell similar stories, and the car seemed to not receive a scratch. Charles was glad the young men were safe and invited them to return any time to rent the Astral Marten car again – that is, any time they would like, except for the second week of each third month of the calendar quarter. The young men said they would certainly rent it again in the near future. They thanked Charles and parted ways.

Chapter 3

The General and the Congressman

By the middle of February, 1971, the Astral Marten had became well known and was very popular, as the word got around about its mysterious capabilities. The car was the coolest experience of the era, and everyone who saw it wanted to drive it, but also purchase it. As word got around, high-ranking military officials and famous celebrities began to rent the car. A General in the Army, a man by the name of Pike, came one day to rent the car, saying he needed to impress a particular congressman and discuss some new Federal bill ideas. "Just politics," he said to Charles, who replied, "Sure, I understand."

All who rented the car, including General Pike, had no clue about the vehicle's ultimate capabilities, which were revealed later, as this story unfolded in the pure superior realm. The Astral Marten had a purpose, which was related to its mysterious beginnings, to gather and record information that would be helpful to all on our planet, Earth in order to save the human consciousness.

Congressman Roy arrived at the small airstrip in town, called Freedom Point. General Pike arrived at the airstrip, driving the Astral Marten, to greet the Congressman and to meet with him inside the car. The

General opened the door for Congressman Roy and invited him to take a seat, and the meeting was underway. General Pike began driving while heading toward the local roads. Congressman Roy began the conversation by making it perfectly clear that he understood the purpose of the meeting, when he stated the following: "I am aware of the reasons you have called me to this meeting. I want to say first, This is a time in our lives when we should be seeking answers to how to liberate all of society on this planet, who are required to exist in a realm of freedom according to a higher law. Our purpose is to disclose the truth as to why wars are a part of the human experience and reality, and the role America will play in the dismantling of this system by not condoning such methods, and not for America to conspire with other countries to wage wars over the course of centuries as we have done."

General Pike replied, "These wars have set the stage for a future strategy – to inadvertently support or to be an active participant in a cause to remain in control of the minds of society." Pike stated that it is an understood, unspoken, international policy that certain countries take turns fighting other countries, while others build up revenue for their next war. "This is a design that has withstood the test of time."

General Pike went into full detail, and explained how the system works. "War serves only one purpose, and that is to hold the perceived reality of societies in a sustained, enslaved existence of total fear, by crippling people's ability to think about anything, except survival, trauma, pain, and bloodlust. It was discovered, long ago, that the emotion of fear causes the mind to shut down, resulting in separation of all humans from the ability to exist in, or to perceive, a realm of a higher standard. Humans are possessive beings. When influenced by materialism, they only know how to define who they are by what they own, or, at a minimum, what they believe they own. This limited reality creates and defines a false reality for people, that then prevents them from discovering who they truly are, which, if they were to apply themselves to what is real, their minds would strengthen, and they would not exist as the limited beings they are in this realm, which is completely made up by men. We would lose our power if they ever figured the power of their own mind!

He then explained the effects of such a system: "When war happens, their emotional reactions dismantle their empowerment to exist in a realm of total love and freedom. Our agenda has always been to keep this realm of reality that we live in separate from the higher realm of reality from above, so as to hide from them their ability to learn of their true purpose and the powers they have had all along, while they are alive in the flesh and in this powerful consciousness. Our success in maintaining control over the world's societies and their minds depends upon this continued weakness of individuals and their lack of knowing how to use their mind. Their ability to find and utilize the limited amount of knowledge that remains available to them, depends upon how they are able rise above the system we have created for the purpose of preventing this very action.

This method was discovered and created thousands of years ago. The act of murder, in the very beginning, not only pushed them out of their original realm, but it also created the experience of anger, pain, and fear. The first murder altered the blueprint of all humans, which, after this first event, now causes their spirits to be required to return here, life after life, until they forgive the violators while they are living in this realm and learn their real purpose. This was discovered long ago, before this planet was invaded by the hijackers from other areas of space."

General Pike continued, "This system replaced our natural spiritual cycles of the Golden, Silver, and Bronze Ages with a (seemingly) never-ending Iron Age of bondage and spiritual enslavement, which happened before the beginning of ancient Egypt. The pyramids on the Giza Plateau mirror Orion's belt of three bright stars, which represent the feminine energy. Those three suns are where most of us are from. The pyramids have one characteristic that separates the two realities. Each pyramid has four sides, and the fourth side represents the Iron Age that was added to the original three cycles. That is the separation of man from the superior realm of the three burning suns that consist of feminine energy. The Iron Age has nothing to do with the feminine realm. Men were never supposed to rule this planet, as they are too destructive! But, this system is what we have inherited, and changing it would create a reality that would not sit well with the facilitators of this realm. For their agenda and purpose, it's good to rule in a reality of total darkness."

In conclusion, General Pike summed up, "Our success in controlling the world's societies has been secured, by creating programs that affect both the reality of the mind and the environment of the mind, down to the neurons in the body, which store the programs of our control in their bodies. When the programs to have uncontrollable SEX, desire MATERIALISM, and to seek POWER are what is stored in their bodies' cells, humans are constantly reminded of the realities we have created, which they perceive as limiting them and which they accept as being real, and which we interpret as their permission to control them. We continue this control by holding all humans in our designed dimension of the false reality we created for them."

Congressman R. J. Roy stated he was not comfortable with the plan to start yet another war. He noted that he would rather find a way to bring peace, that we must attempt to restore the reality back to what it was, before man decided to break away from our original realm and reality (after the first murder), and that we have a moral and ethical obligation to our own kind to do so. "We exist with two species of humans here, ones that are of peace and originate from the three sister suns, and the ones who are not from there, which are the ones who strive for war, such as yourself. General Pike, are you one of them? Are you one of the invading species of this planet that arrived here, long ago? Or are you a human who voluntarily and knowingly assists the invaders in their agenda of imposing a controlling net on the human species, which prevents the people from accessing their original realm?"

General Pike was greatly taken aback. He had expected complicity, and he did not want to hear those words spoken by Congressman R. J. Roy – or by anyone. The Congressman further stated, "The United States is in a state of panic – about war, jobs, the economy, and the education of their children. I am not about to be the one to present such a dangerous idea, which carries the possibility of getting the world into the next war, a war that would erase source knowledge from society. Society is getting closer to learning the truth, and quite frankly, I do not want to be on the wrong side in this movement."

General Pike angrily stated, "This war will happen, and I will do whatever it takes to get it done!"

The General and the Congressman finished their day's agenda, and General Pike returned the car in less than twenty-four hours. He noted to Charles, "What a nice ride this car is, and it handles and performs like a dream!" He also inquired whether Charles would ever consider selling the car?

Charles replied without hesitation "No, not for all the money in the world." Charles thanked the General for his compliment, as he parked the car back into its spot, where it would await the next customer.

Spring was approaching, and the car had already been rented daily by many high ranking officials in government, including individuals from the CIA and FBI, all of whom offered enormous amounts of money to purchase it. Charles explained, "My brother created and named this car. This car is very unique in its mysterious design. It seems as though it is as alive as the humans who drive it. I tell all of them the very same thing, 'I can't sell it, and this is my brother, Jackson's, car.'"

Charles thought to himself, "Time is moving forward rapidly. Soon it will be the tenth day of March, the third month of this quarter, and Lady Jamis will be here to go on her next adventure for three days, with a car that is very special to her, for reasons I don't know. I do know that I have made more money renting this one car out to the locals, than I have ever made selling all the other vehicles."

Chapter 4

The Chancellor is Dining,
But the Car is Listening

During the following week, Marcy Chancellor, the founder of the charity "Color Works for Orphaned Children," and the surviving heir to the Chancellor fortune, reserved the Astral Marten to entertain one of her top sponsors. She arranged for dinner at the prestigious restaurant "The Chancellor is Dining." Marcy reserved a private room and arranged for a gourmet menu to be prepared and ready for her guest. The meeting was to discuss generating more funds for her charity. She had parked the Astral Marten just outside the French doors, by her table, and was within eye view of the car. Marcy was unaware of the capabilities of the car.

The sponsor laughed as he made light of the fact that most charities serve a great purpose: "They allow the wealthiest people to avoid paying taxes [because we can reduce our taxable income by making large donations to charities and foundations], while we experience all the luxuries at our donors' cost, because their donations basically sustain our lifestyle, free of charge!" He went on to say that the donations are so that the weak [meaning ordinary folks who donate] will fill the world with sadness and give all they can to us! He explained that he, also, needed to donate money to avoid paying too much in taxes. He asked, "Shall I write the check for $300,000?"

Marcy smiled as she responded to his generosity, "Yes, of course, Darling! That deserves a toast!" As she raised her glass of champagne, she said "Here's to the little people who keep me in business," which was a reference to the orphaned children.

She went on to explain how she started her charity, many years ago, right out of college, and that within six months, she had married her wealthy, billionaire, husband, Jack. She explained that she and her sister were the heirs to the Chancellor fortune, and that her parents died in a car crash, when she and her sister were young girls. "We were both raised in a prestigious boarding school." She continued, "We figured out this system quite well. People like you and me rest on the shoulders of the weak and ignorant."

The meeting was a success, and Marcy and her sponsor wrapped up their meeting and returned to the Astral Marten. While further discussing their next meeting, Marcy delivered her guest back to his hotel, where they mutually said, "Until we meet next time, my friend." Marcy hugged him tightly and thanked him for his generosity. She had no further business and felt no further need for the Astral Marten, so she returned it to the lot and surrendered the vehicle back to its owner.

Charles greeted Marcy and inquired how she had liked the car? She was rather smug in her reply, "My goodness, it's just a car! It's not like it's a spaceship! It rides nicely, and it did not break down." Charles was shocked at her demeanor and reaction. Nonetheless, he thanked her and invited her to rent it again in the near future. Marcy replied, "I will, when another sponsor with big bucks donates more revenue to my charity." Charles just looked at her in a perplexed manner. He wanted to think of her as a nicer person, such as Lady Jamis. After dealing with Marcy, he was looking forward to seeing Lady Jamis. Then, all of a sudden, Marcy turned to Charles, thanked him for his kindness, and said, "The car is super cool!" Charles cracked a huge grin to Marcy, as she winked at him and slowly turned away from her view of him.

Chapter 5

The Mysterious Lady Returns
to the Old Abandoned House

Charles thought to himself, "The time has arrived, and tomorrow is the tenth of June, the third month in this quarter, and Lady Jamis will be here at 9:00 a.m. I have had several disappointed clients, who wanted to rent this mysterious car, today and the next few days. I had to inform them that it was already prepaid, in advance, for the next three days, and that it would be available on the fourteenth of this month. Well, it's a quarter to nine, now. I had better get the gates opened for Jamis. She promptly pulls in at exactly nine o'clock, on the dot. I already have the car pulled out and ready for her departure. I wonder where she will go? I am so curious to know, and I hesitate to ask, but I ask, anyway, out of sheer curiosity."

"Good morning, Lady Jamis. Where will your adventures carry you this time?"

She smiled and said, "Oh, it's a secret. But, I promise, I will take very good care of your baby, while she is in my care."

Charles responded, "Oh, okay, I understand. I am not concerned at all about the car. This car has had many near accidents, but always seems to come out of it unscathed."

Lady Jamis looked perplexed, with regard to these facts, and said to Charles, "Really? Well, that is comforting to know."

Lady Jamis placed her travel case in the trunk, slid into the driver's seat, and she pressed her small hand over the censor to start the car. Now heading out from the car lot, she waved her petite hand to offer a gesture of farewell to Charles, and called out, "See you in three days," as she drove out of sight.

Charles said out loud to himself, "Whoever her husband is, he is quite a lucky lad. She is such a sweet, beautiful lady."

Lady Jamis once again traveled down that long, desolate, country road, which leads into the next township. She had yet to make it to the next town in that car. On this trip, she purposely sought out the long driveway, which leads to the old abandoned house that sits a distance from the highway. Now that she was driving the Marten, she easily found the old boarded up house, and parked the car behind the house, as she did once before. Upon entering the house, she headed straight for the back bedroom, to the very same spot she went to the last time – this time to find her glasses, which were on the floor, right where she left them the last time. She wrote notes and added more knowledge to the already existing letters and pictures that were stored under the floorboards. She was entrusted with a gift and a purpose, and she learned many things that are very important to mankind's future.

It is significant that Jamis was able to recall her conscious memory of what happened during her last trip to the old house, with the Astral Marten. Because she was able to remember, she has realized her purpose and her unique opportunity to serve others. The time she spends in that old, abandoned house is priceless. Lady Jamis has been on a mission to seek the real knowledge of the Universe and the world. She has advanced her mind and has grown to be a free-minded spirit, who knows what the free will really means. She has learned that the world has been programmed to think, live, and even act in certain way, a way that conflicts with what is correct, according to the superior realm. She has discovered the deception of the false reality, which General Pike described, while he was driving the Astral Marten. She enjoyed much success during the next few days, during her next adventure with the Astral Marten. The time Jamis spends in the presence of this vehicle brings her another step closer to her mission being complete. The information she and the car record and collect is building quickly. The day will arrive when she puts everything into motion, so that everyone may experience and learn. The dream state she enters, while she is in the house, is how she has obtained all the knowledge she has.

At the end of her three days with the car, the time came for her to return the Astral Marten back to

Charles. She arrived on schedule, and Charles greeted her, as he does every time. The paperwork awaited her signature, as she reached for her reading glasses, so she could see properly to sign the paper.

Charles asked, "Do you have any stories to share with me?"

Jamis answered, "I am sorry, but I don't. I find when I drive this car I somehow become lost inside myself." She noted further, "I can't quite explain it. I enter into a realm that I can't explain. I am safe and have never been in danger."

Charles responded, "That is fascinating to know. I have never heard anyone give such a report."

Jamis thanked him, as usual, and confirmed that she would see him in three months. She shook his hand and thanked him for being so kind and helpful. Charles was blushing that she was holding his hand, even if it was only to shake it. Jamis said again, "See you in three months," as she got into her own vehicle. She blew a kiss to the Astral Marten and drove away.

Chapter 6

The Movie Producer's Shocking Lunch

For the next three months, it was back to regular business for the Astral Marten. Charles' next customer was a big time Hollywood producer, who heard about this unusual, unique car that could only be rented. Charles had the twenty-four-hour contract ready for Reddick Polano to sign. Reddick arrived and explained he was looking to entertain a few other producers, who were to assist him in his next film, "The Sexual Encounter of a Youth."

Charles noted, "That is a very unusual title for a film."

Reddick responded, "It is to auto-suggest to the viewers to engage more in sexual activity."

Charles changed the subject by explaining the features of the car, which included that it does not require any fuel and has no gas tank or ignition. He said, "There is no need to panic about being stranded in the rural parts of this area of the state. There are no speed limits in these parts, and the Astral Marten has no limit on its speedometer." Charles explained a little about the reason why the car was here and how his brother created it. He ended the conversation with an open-ended question, asking whether Reddick had any questions about the car?

Reddick impatiently replied, "No, I do not," because he really wanted to get going, to meet his two producers at the train station on time.

The two producers, Thomas Clark and Sidney Welsh, arrived by train from Los Angeles, and Reddick was waiting patiently to pick them up. The three held a conversation about the next film, until they came within sight of the car, and then they stopped and stared at the Astral Marten. The two men were speechless, until Thomas asked, "Where on Earth did you find a car like this?"

Reddick responded by saying, "I read about it in one of the science magazines I subscribe to. It has become a popular experience to try. I thought it would be fun and a great addition to our meeting."

Both producers were amazed with the details that were shared; especially that it was a fuel-less vehicle. Both men noted, "Wow! This car has some type of atmosphere about it! The air is crisp and clean, the scent is unusually pleasant, and it does not have the new scent of a new car, but it looks and feels as though it just came off the showroom floor." Reddick agreed totally with them both.

The engine just quietly sung, as it sped down the highway. They were heading to the only upscale restaurant in those parts, "The Chancellor is Dining." Reddick reserved the same private room of the restaurant that Marcy, the founder of Color Works Charity, did previously, and parked the car just outside of the French double doors, again, just within eye-view.

The men placed their cocktail orders and proceeded to discuss business. Reddick went over the purpose of the meeting. He explained that he was a close friend with several high-ranking government officials, and that he was approached with some new discoveries that required top ranking producers in the movie industry of American movies, to set the stage for these discoveries to operate on the workings of the minds of people.

"Our job is to create and produce more films that promote increased sexual activity. The reasons why, will blow your mind! When I was briefed, I could hardly believe what their research revealed. The discovery was: the more we auto-suggest and produce films, both on the general television and in private films, encouraging females to engage more in sexual activity, and this limits her ability to ever overpower a man. Women are taught to believe they hold power over the male species by their sexuality, and, in a sense, they do, but the real agenda is to keep them active with having orgasms. It has been discovered that both males and females lose their inner power with each orgasm! I was shocked when I was informed of this discovery. Apparently, this is how the system maintains itself and is able to keep society at a minimum sustained standard, so as to prevent people from connecting to their higher self. This discovery has been known for thousands of years, but, until recently, it was not fully understood. We have been guaranteed a great incentive – to be paid handsomely to change the course of society and exploit women in a way that leads them to believe they are very powerful, when really all we are doing is draining them of their energy and limiting them of their powers."

Both Thomas and Sidney were quiet, and sat, with a blank look on their faces, for about two or three minutes. Thomas was first to speak, and he said outright, "I am not sure I want to be a part of this project. It seems to me, that if I were a part of it, I would have to face a higher council, once my cycle ends. I am not going to do something here and now, just because it's legal, when it's actually unethical, and cause myself to carry a burden of guilt for the rest of my life." Thomas said further, "I will not ever look at my wife the same way, ever again, knowing our acts of love are damaging to us both. No, Reddick! I am out of this experiment."

Sidney continued to sit in a position of stunned silence. Reddick said, "Come on, guys, this has been going on for thousands of years. This is why the female is limited, and this is about keeping men in control."

Thomas interjected, "I want no control, and I want to honor what is naturally correct! If women were to be leaders then it should be that way. We have no right to alter or manipulate what should be and that which is lawfully correct."

The waiter arrived to take their order, and their meals were served within a reasonable time.

Sidney finally joined in and supported Thomas, in his reaction to the forecast of the plan. He said that he also wanted nothing to do with this dangerous and unethical idea. Reddick warned them, that they are "walking away from a great business opportunity."

Thomas retorted, "This is not business, this is people's minds we are talking about! The removing of the very foundations of a cooperative society." Thomas then stated that, in the future, he would focus more on educational films.

Reddick warned again, "You must not use this discovery for the bases of your films, to reveal this to people. They will murder you, before you could open your mouth."

Thomas sighed deeply, with great frustration. He asked Reddick, "How could you be a part of such a scheme, to undermine both male and female, and sleep at night?"

Reddick replied by saying he is a sex addict, and further noted, "I do my part by slipping into every woman I possibly can. I realize my actions may not be the most ethical, but one thing is for sure – it is my choice, and regardless, I will return in the next life being drawn to the very same experiences. I do know there is no death, and until I find my higher purpose, I am going to continue to live and keep with the current system."

The meeting was not at all what Reddick had planned. Thomas and Sidney were great friends of his, and he respected their reasons to not want to be a part of this venture, but he was disappointed. The three top producers finished their meals, and each man paid a visit to the restroom, before the long ride back to the train station.

Reddick, Thomas, and Sidney were soon back in the Marten, *in route* to the train station. The ride was silent, and there seemed to be nothing further to discuss. Reddick was not upset, but was now on the hunt for the right producers to assist him in his mission. The men arrived back at the train station and said their farewells to Reddick. They did not wish him good luck on his upcoming project. They shook hands and boarded the train.

Reddick sat back, inside the Astral Marten, feeling slightly confused. He could not understand why. He felt like something was trying to communicate with him. Just a strange feeling had come over him. He drove as quickly as possible to return the car back to Charles. After he arrived at the car lot, he parked the Astral Marten, and said to Charles, "What a wonderful vehicle!"

Charles asked, "How did the meeting go?"

Reddick replied, "Not at all as I wanted it to. I have a lot to consider, and I need to get my priorities in order. This is going to sound strange, but something about this car was making me feel like it was trying to communicate with me. I can't explain it exactly. All I know is, I was in deep thought about my meeting with my two producer friends, and it seemed as though, once I was alone in the car, I could sense something, but nothing bad. Well anyway, I thank you so much! I will spread the word to my friends to give this a try."

Charles thanked him for sharing his experience and stated, "I have heard similar stories from others." He welcomed Reddick to come back any time, except during the time that it is reserved, every three months.

Reddick signed the return slip and said, "Farewell, until next time."

Reddick was now back in his own car, he paused for a few minutes, before he drove off. He stared at the Astral Marten and said, "What were you trying to tell me?" Then, he proceeded on his way, and slowly drifted out of view of the Astral Marten.

Charles soon became busy with reporters, who requested more interviews about the mysterious car. The list was quickly growing, of people reserving the car. The Astral Marten became a celebrity, more popular than the highest paid actor or actress. Charles' days were busier than ever, yet he dared a pleasant thought:

"The time is rapidly approaching for the beautiful Lady Jamis to arrive. Tomorrow is the tenth day of September, the third month of this quarter, and she will be arriving, like clockwork, to rent the car for three days, for the third time." Charles arrives early to prepare for Jamis' arrival at exactly 9:00 a.m. sharp.

Chapter 7

Jamis Reveals What the Car is Really Up To

Charles had a blushing smile on his face, when Lady Jamis stepped out of her car. She greeted him with a friendly, "Hello," and inquired, "Why the huge smile?"

He replied, "I am so glad to see you."

Jamis smiled, and replied the very same. Then, she said, "I have some great news! I am an expectant mother! I am just past my first trimester."

Charles was so happy to hear that! He said, "Congratulations to you and your husband!"

Jamis responded with, "Thank you. We were shocked. We had tried for years, and finally had given up on it happening. But, we must have done something right for a change!"

Jamis conveyed she will keep the schedule they have kept, for rental of the Marten, except when she reaches her last trimester of her pregnancy. Charles had no problem at all with that. Jamis thanked him for honoring their agreement. She said she and her husband "are so into the science of reproduction of life! It is so amazing! We know everything we say and do affects our baby. I have been reading so much out loud. I can't wait to sit in the car and let my baby experience the Astral Marten!"

Charles said, "You must give me a full report of the baby's reaction, once you return from your adventure!"

Jamis replied, "I surely will."

She placed her overnight bag in the trunk, sat in the driver's seat of the Astral Marten, and waved goodbye, as she drove away.

Jamis drove the car, this time with another occupant, down that long country road. Her baby moved around during the whole ride, as though she were playing on a playground. Jamis knew the Astral Marten had to be the cause of her baby's burst of energy! She made it to the old house, where, this time, she will share her knowledge in the presence of her unborn baby. Jamis knows her baby will record all her actions during her visit in the old house. Jamis has no need to pull out her glasses, because she knows that, within that house, her vision is perfect. She will deliver new documents to the secret hiding place. She will read until it is time to leave. The time will pass quickly, as it always does, and she will become aware, as though she were being signaled, to find that it is time to prepare to head back home, in order to return the Astral Marten.

But, before Lady Jamis returns the car, she is ready for you to learn all that she has learned, and she is

going to share with you why she reserves the Astral
Marten every quarter, for three days.

The car everyone had been driving was truly
unique, in ways no one could have ever imagined or
suspected. It was created to have the capability to record
all conversations of everyone who spoke in its presence,
within 1,000 feet of its computers. The Astral Marten
exist in such a way; any device created by man, in his
limited reality of existence, cannot destroy it. Its body is
made of a titanium-like material that comes from another
dimension of existence, but which takes on the look of
commonly known metals that are found here, on planet
Earth. It is capable of tracking flights, military, combat,
commercial, and private vehicles, and any nuclear
missiles, anywhere, any time.

Lady Jamis was visually drawn to its energy and
sleek design. The car recorded her conversation with her
husband, while they waited at the traffic light. The car
responded by sending a signal to her mind, which then
recorded into her neurons within her cells, and within all
molecules in her body, which, in turn, became a
vibrational antenna, that elevated her desire to see the
car up close, intensifying as hours passed.

Lady Jamis entered the other dimension just
moments after being in the car. She soon realized that
the old house could only be viewed while she is in the
Astral Marten. She could not have seen that house from
the road in her personal vehicle. The house existed as a
depot for the other dimension on planet Earth. The long

driveway was winding and narrow, and the house was hidden from sight of all humans in this dimension of reality. The common person could not see it from the road! Because of the Astral Marten, she saw the house at the end of the driveway from within the vortex of her mind. The house had been there all along, in its own dimension, and only when she was physically inside the Astral Marten could she see it. The car caused her to be able to do this the first time she rented it.

The car, having this type of influence, proved how easily the human species could be controlled and influenced, because our minds are weak and are very susceptible to outside influence. Jamis has strengthened her mind, and now uses her own Free Will to enter the vortex that is located in her mind. The very important and secret documents were intended for her eyes-only. Any other humans traveling that road will never see the old frame house, just as Jamis never saw the house, before she drove the Astral Marten. Yet, not all drivers of the car have been able to see the house, only those whom the car intends to see it, which, so far, has included only Jackson and Lady Jamis.

By causing her to go to the house, the first time, the car was able to educate Lady Jamis about who she really was. As she read the papers under the floorboards, she learned why humans were enslaved: an outside entity invaded this planet long ago, with the purpose of creating a false, faceless entity (that is nothing more than a concept), that many people would accept as a real god, and would murder and sacrifice each other to honor this faceless entity, changing the one peaceful feminine utopia into a battleground of one man against another. By keeping all beings in a state of chaos, with people fighting and murdering each other, it was too easy to enslave them, and evil humans colluded with the evil invaders from space, to create a false reality overlay, which uses the movie screens within our minds to convince humans it is reality. This false reality overlay is difficult to see past and to get out of our minds. Humans tend to believe that what they experience is real, and so, they believed the false reality to be real, never suspecting the invasive manipulation. The humans' own government once used this fake entity to secure control over the population, but, now, it regulates their minds by creating mind programs, controlling the interpretation and meaning of all events, so that situations are taken on as realities and seem to be so real, so natural, but which absolutely are false and are contrived – imposed. Their success has led them to no longer desire to use gods to manipulate people, and they are currently in the process of removing them from all government offices.

Lady Jamis discovered all this during her first visit to the abandoned house. She was required to read all of the notes that were left for her. During each visit, the instructions communicated to her to act upon her newly discovered purpose, and this is when she had run quickly and got in the car, which she would not remember doing and would experience as a lapse of missing time. This would lead her to be the bravest woman she could ever have imagined herself to be, because, during those times, that car returned to its original dimension of superior existence. The newly recorded data had to be transferred to the main computer in the other dimension, and the car could not return without a driver.

The purpose for transferring all the data it had gathered, up to that point, from all humans who had rented the car, was to help all humans who resided on Earth to overcome their programming by the outside invaders (who were assisted by greedy, power-hungry humans). When humans are able to overcome their programming, it will eliminate and prevent what was about to happen to the planet Earth from space. The twelve energy vortexes in Earth's invisible portholes, which is an alien created, planetary, energy grid, are rapidly drawing a massive neutron star to this planet, which would cause the destruction of our entire Solar system. The governments of the world have kept this event a tight secret from the humans of Earth. Their only concern is keeping the humans stifled and controlled, so as to prevent them from rising above the concepts of Taxes and Commerce, Fear and Poverty, Injury, Death, and War. These concepts rob many from finding their purpose. They are there to create burden, by blocking humans from experiencing real freedom.

The car was designed to seek out and read the cells in humans that were created by programs, such as the ones described above, so that its actual creators in the other dimension (not Jackson) may find a method, that does not violate humans' free will, of deprogramming them, so that, when their cycle ends, they can return their spirit back to its higher realm of reality. In order to find the correct method to help humans, and learn of how the humans were enslaved by their own governments, this car became the asset needed to correct the current system of control, while creating a workable plan to counter and forever block the current reality overlay, that was designed by an invading entity, who was portrayed as a male god in all religions, from succeeding any further.

In order to accomplish the gathering of this information, the car had to scan the body cells in each human, that contain the programmed information that makes up their reality and impacts their consciousness, records the data from enough humans, from all walks of life, for a broad collecting of information, as to discover the design of how the control was implemented, and to discover the foundations of the very system that has been practiced and carried out – what we refer to as a government – that was supposed to serve and protect its people, and not to commit the barbaric acts of violence which governments have. These acts have served to sever the lifeline of humans from their human souls, which reside in the same dimension that the Astral Marten is from, and which is far more powerful than the dimension of reality man has created.

When the data has been gathered, and a plan has been put into place by beings in the superior dimension, this will ultimately lead to the rulers of Earth having to stand down and relinquish their control over the humans' consciousness. To access one's soul in another dimension, one must have the right knowledge, which has also been blocked or hidden. Once the people have this knowledge, the false reality will have no power over them, and the current rulers of Earth will also have no power over humans. This program, the false reality, was created strictly for the rulers' own personal gain, by way of the business dealings of financial institutions, tax collecting agencies, a consumer (spending, materialistic) economy, policies of constant war, and continual threat of imprisonment, death, or torture for those who dare to be non-compliant. These have contributed to the creation of a commerce of fear, which condemns freedom and true human purpose.

The Astral Marten car was a high tech computer in disguise! This car ran from energy, whose source cannot be detected with the naked eye or any device man has in his possession. Its inner workings were designed like a spacecraft, that was designed to decode and read the cells that makes up the human reality, that then becomes the collective (shared) and individual experience, by folding invisibly into the environment, that originates from the mind, that is influenced by government. Keep in mind that this vehicle recorded all elements of our existence, with regard to the DNA of all who were within a 1,000 feet in a radius of its computer's signal.

Its endless database is continually eternal and has the full story of the past and the knowledge of the Ages. The Astral Marten has a full handle on how everything repeats itself, both good and bad, from creation to destruction, in this experience we call consciousness. The seemingly endless spiral repeats itself, until we rise to a higher purpose of thinking and knowing, except when this process is interrupted or broken by an evil overlay of the true reality, by insidiously manipulating people's minds.

The information of each person, who was recorded by the car, along with the information from notes taken by Jackson and Jamis, allowed the beings from Atlantis, who exist in the superior dimension, and who created the Astral Marten, to better understand what would be necessary in order to help us all to learn what is required, so that we may be granted to return to our pure realm of love and freedom after we complete this life cycle. The Astral Marten discovered that our experience of the sexual climax actually depletes our knowledge and allows the separation from our higher self. Both men's and women's senses are dulled after climaxing during sex, but there are spiritual consequences for this, that the rulers of Earth do not want us to know, because it keeps us bound to them. This was important information for the Atlanteans to find out, so that they could help us.

In addition to top-down causes, such as the movie producer's goal to affect people with his movies, this car also had the ability to detect the effects upon mere mortal humans, whose experience was only limitation and lack, due to the influence over their minds. To help the people, it must become possible to reverse and alter the current programs that are infested within the body cells, where each stores the false reality as programs into each human body. This is what creates what the people believe to be real – their personal experience. The solution is to teach the Real Science of how the mind holds all the answers to what is right, as compared to what has gone wrong. Understanding these facts would be necessary, before one could convert the bad cells into the type of knowledge that activates the mind to think more freely and to bring to the surface the encrypted knowledge, which are embedded ancient codes within human cells. The mind must be introduced to a new way of existing, before the encrypted code may be discovered, which is found within all cellular databases of all humans of all cultures.

Once enough data was discovered and gathered, it would become evident, to the Astral Marten car and to the others in the dimension of the car's origin, what the necessary steps that are needed to correct the man-created reality. These steps, once implemented, would need to cause the knowledge to come to the surface of the mind of each born mortal of how to free the will and how to learn the science of how to apply the mind, so that it is capable of much more than it has been experiencing, until now, or been trained to do.

The truth should finally be disclosed to the populations by their own authorities. This includes the science of how the body carries little pockets of cells that are created by all experiences, from past lives that carry into the present time and that the cells which vibrate the most, create signals that contain and maintain all programs and realities, whether they may be correct or incorrect, and how these signals either enhance the environment or dismantle the environment that then re-influences the mind, via feedback, also known as "results/consequences," to create more incorrect cells within the human vessel, promoting such grave experiences, such as fear and lack and very little of the emotion of LOVE.

The Astral Marten discovered that both wealthy and poor were running on the wrong knowledge and were creating wrong cells. It also discovered that very little of the experience of real love was among the cells in humans it recorded. Love is the foundation and food for the strength and survival of the spirit, so that a human may receive the correct knowledge that harvests real freedom. The super-antenna array structures found all over the world, created by men and governments, were carefully set up in geographical patterns, for the purpose of creating and sustaining the realities of both, those who seemed to be educated in these matters, as well as the uneducated.

The car succeeded in its mission to seek out and discover the functions designed by man, which were created to develop a reality of limitation and enslavement. The discovery of this information had to be done in a certain fashion, so that the obtaining of it did not violate Universal laws, the car was programmed to listen, record, and perform a certain level of analysis.

The governments do not care about Universal Laws, and do not function under the superior laws of the

Universal Federation; instead, they have gone to extremes – to convey information that is actually false and damning to all members of society. The purpose, of course, is to hold on to people's spirits under a limited false control, in order to ensure that ignorance is practiced daily, twenty-four hours every day, 365 days a year. Denying source knowledge, for both wealthy and poor, guarantees that the spirit of each soul returns to be reborn as a mortal being, born into slavery as a result of not knowing the truth, trapped in a false dimension. This serves the rulers, because they gain from the physical enslavement, and it serves the space invaders, who feed on the trauma of the oppressed like food. Now, all who fail to capture the knowledge are required to reincarnate back here, returning to relive and to follow the same program as the previous life, within newly created paradigms of illusions by the designers, as many times as are needed, until, eventually, the chances run out, or the person learns the proper knowledge and breaks the cycle of ignorance.

It had also been acknowledged that there were beings on this planet, who were aliens originating from another place, and certainly from another time. Aliens were cloned, specifically so that they would be able to blend in with the more spiritual beings, the humans. But, the clones were missing one important part of existing in the same consciousness; the missing code is the ability to love. These beings are easily pinpointed, because they have limited range of emotion, no emotional depth or compassion, and no regard for life; they engage in dangerous plots to rule and to limit societies, as a sort of game that they enjoy; they also abuse wildlife, domestic animals, and humans that are around them. These beings are all over the planet and in all societies, blending in as everyone else. Specifically a female will run for office as President that mirrors the description above.

Once enough data had been gathered, the civilization of light that is located within the dimension of the Astral Marten, would receive this data, analyze it, and create a plan to help the spirited beings to break free of the constraints of control by these impostor, look-alike humans, who invited themselves to our planet. The civilization of Orion's Belt is connected to the beings of spirit, who are trapped here on Earth. A great example to illustrate this situation is when Americans have been captured by militants in another country, and become Prisoners of War (POW). Now, open your mind and consider the mission of the Astral Marten. It is here to seek legal methods to free the spiritual beings that originated long ago from the star system of Orion's Belt. They are planning a rescue, by way of hundreds of galactic spaceships, to aid in the saving of, not the human body, but the human consciousness. The spirit is connected to the consciousness, and together they are what make it humanly possible to exist in a physical body.

Our planet, Earth, had already sought out a remedy, and had created a black energy that is heading now towards our planet earth. The purpose of this dark energy is for the true humans (not the hybrids or the aliens) to breath it into their lungs, causing the cells of knowledge to awaken.

The dark energy, while not affecting the aliens, is able to separate the spirits belonging to the feminine creator from the impostors of the alien race, who are cloned, and those who are humans, but who are intentionally causing or supporting all the confusion and enslavement.

This dark energy is tasteless, and its only purposes are to awaken the cells of knowledge of spirited humans and to activate the emotion of love, which will free all humans from the spiritual and physical darkness, that is from the civilization of darkness, where the aliens originated from a very long time ago. This is why this mission of the Astral Marten has been so important.

The possibility that the planet Earth would be compromised, which did happen before, means that the humans of spirit became blinded to the truth of their original origins, which is that they were brought here when their last planet was destroyed, which is why there is the asteroid belt within the system of our planets.

The Astral Marten made the astounding discovery that all wars were created, planned, and executed, so as to keep humans so busy with trauma and with destructive emotions and acts, that they would not apply themselves to discover the knowledge they needed for their freedom. Further, all religions that were supported by all levels of governments, supported the false reality and the control paradigm, teaching the people to believe in male 'gods,' superior over everyone and all aspects of life, so as to further keep all humans stifled, and to prevent them from evolving, because they were taught falsely that freedom must be fought for, when the fighting leads to further enslavement, and when true freedom has been available to all spirited humans the whole time. This Freedom is called love, and it includes the power to forgive, that molds the free will.

War ensures the continuance of slavery, and it has provided the deceptive power that keeps the false reality in place. The true mechanism of this, which even the military supporters who encourage soldiers to enlist would never believe, is that the soldiers' real purpose is not so especially to fight the enemies across the waters, which they do, but to aid in confining the people there to exist in a limited reality, perpetuating their ignorance by disrupting their lives, which causes the people in that land to have to focus on mere survival, so that only a few advance to the next level, once the current cycle has ended.

The Astral Marten has also time-traveled into the future, specifically to see what lies ahead and how it will unfold, when the correct solution is decided upon by the light beings. By doing this, the Marten has also discovered what solution works.

Before the twelve vortexes (of the alien energy grid system) of the Earth self-destruct, there will be massive loss of, not of life, but a massive loss of consciousness, and the planet will be left in a shambles, the ecosystem and the atmosphere destroyed, which will then lead to a massive loss of life. The car's report from the future yielded evidence of a system in place that was created by technology from a dimension that supplies the evil humans, who help to create the reality of lack in most people's minds. This technology, utilized by the actions of these evil men and women, not only serves to undermine discovery of the knowledge that there is a true reality beyond the one they work so hard to create, but their agenda is also to prevent future spacecraft from entering this atmosphere (such as the rescue ships).

Soldiers must be aware of the fact of the Science of where and what their consciousness last recorded in previous lives, and they are drawn to the very same experience recorded in them in the past. The Astral Marten discovered that where the spirited human last spent his or her last moments in a live consciousness setting, will be the place that they are reborn again. This is why so many humans are seeking to return where they once lived and recorded in their cells, before they participated in acts of war, fighting for a cause that is all man created and designed. These men and women are blind sided of knowing real Science. If they understood where they Parrish is where they will start the next life. This means in all those 3rd world countries limited by rule and power. They will become as dreamers to desire to live where conditions are greater like, being an American again. The system is set up to prevent the soldiers to return to America in the next cycle in their brand new disguise.

The humans must master the science of creation and Alchemy, and finally see that each human is energy and cannot be destroyed or owned, but they can certainly be lost, due to the false beliefs that serve, not a higher purpose, but cause a waste of a beautiful consciousness. If what is required is not mastered, while in this current consciousness, while we are alive inside of a body of flesh, all that has been correctly discovered has been a waste of precious time. The multiple Universes are counting on the Astral Marten to impact the humans to wake up and to seek the knowledge, before the events begin to unfold, and it is too late. Life can and will be again, as energy will always exist. The slow and long process of evolution -- why chance it? Learn real knowledge and Science that will lead to the discovery of the power of LOVE. The Astral Marten originated from a realm of this power, which is love. It knows the exact procedure needed in order to correct the patterns that have been created and used by man.

All governments would fear the purpose of the Astral Marten, if they knew why it existed in their created reality. They believe that their technology programs will prevent the rescue by the alien forces, who have responded to the signal sent by the Astral Marten of light, and who are *en route* from the city of Atlantis, which very much still exists, and is where the Astral Marten is from. Their plan is to prevent penetration of our planetary space by the rescue ships, by generating ionic waves, but they will lose because of their own darkness and weak power, by the lawless concepts they practice. The ionic microwave signal can place a shield around the entire planet; it does disintegrate or knock power out from objects (such as birds or jet planes) that fly near or into it, and when it activates as a shield, the energy will be death or horrible pain to all humans on the ground and in the air. However, the spacecrafts will be able to safely and successfully enter Earth's atmosphere, uninhibited by the HAARP toy man has created. The ships are made of energy. Energy passing through energy will not destruct.

What will be affected, when the ionic shield is activated, are our commercial aircraft, which will lose power and drop like flies out of the skies. The satellites will be destroyed, causing Internet crashes and no cell phone signals. This is why governments and airline companies returned the battleships back to manual navigation. They once had all warships connected to wireless satellites. The government spent billions in the 1990s to return the ships' navigational systems back to manual communication and radar.

The dynamics are very much real, and what is coming cannot be stopped, but what can be done is that humans can learn what is required to graduate to the next level and dimension of reality and move, once and for all, out of this current reality, that is man created. The fact that humans know of the concepts of yin and yang, but have never really understood the two fully, has placed all humans at a disadvantage. Yin is the powerful loving feminine energy, and while yang is the active, protective, male energy. The yang energy currently exists out of role, contrary to its original purpose and function, and is being used to willingly sacrifice universal law through a paradigm of total domination, for the illusion of power over others. It is a false paradigm within the reality overlay that the dominators have created, in their own minds and in the minds of other spirited humans, that has caused limitation to be transferred into their cells, with the result that they are convinced this limited life is the only way things can be. Humans at lower levels of their hierarchy, as well as those who are unaware of this choice, misuse yang energy to enslave and destroy, instead of build and protect, which affects the entire population of this planet.

There are two civilizations, one is a civilization of divinity of light and the other is a civilization of darkness, and both have interest in our planet. The divine light of Atlantis is seeking freedom for the souls created in the likeness of a superior, feminine God, the source energy, while the civilization that is also present here on earth, the darkness, has a purpose to inflict suffering by creating a conflict of reality that is not in the likeness of our source. Our source is a powerful energy beyond anyone's comprehension. These two civilizations have not gods, but leaders of male and female. One civilization exists in the light while the other exists in the darkness.

The male leader of darkness is tied into all governments, organized religion, and the large banking system. The religions of this planet use the divinity of light to deceive the humans into believing they are representing the trinity of God that reflects in both male and female energies. A God, not any one person, can be described as ever existing in the flesh, besides the born Messiah of the Hebrews, who represents the feminine realm of love and wisdom, the master of forgiveness.

The churches in Europe and around the world represent the dark civilization, as they have contributed to the murder of millions over the course of over two thousand years. They have committed these acts to preserve their agenda, using a false entity, and calling him God, as a tool to carry out their ill intent to blindside the world by the use of death and the fear of dying to manipulate and control people, and raping young children (boys) for centuries. It is obvious to see, Love is not their agenda, and this should be easily identified. Love has been a huge missing part of the Lost Encrypted Knowledge. Love does conquer all, and it is the glue of creation. The light was not created by the darkness. It was a willful choice on the part of the individuals who instill darkness instead of teaching love or practice its powerful energy, which could result from mastering the real power of love.

If one believes his or her government will serve and protect them, then that is a sad assumption to believe. The knowledge has been purposely kept from all, by governments, religions, and by commerce systems, and this is because the bottom line is they care not what your birthright is, which is to be free to expand your mind by experiencing the laws of science, but instead they falsely believe they have a tight grip of ownership on all minds of society. What they are unaware of is, they will be blindsided by their own lack and ignorance. The truth will ultimately not be denied.

Chapter 8

Where Did the Astral Marten Come From?

In this chapter, Jamis will share with you how the Astral Marten came to be. This car is from another dimension and had a mission to accomplish on this Planet Earth. This mission required different humans (Jackson, Lady Jamis and Harmony) to use the powerful abilities of their minds.

This was a very important mission for the benefit of the human consciousness, because the car originated from the realm of the highest intelligence of the mind, a created and designed civilization of divine light called Atlantis, the car was originally a spaceship. It was scheduled to land precisely when the intended receiver would be in the right place and was able to observe its entry into our atmosphere. The time was 1947, in Roswell, New Mexico. The space vessel touched down on the farm of the parents of Jackson and Charles Pearce.

Jackson was surveying his parents' land, in order to expand the area for planting more crops, to yield more food for surrounding states. He was the first one on the scene, to encounter the unidentified disc that just landed on the very area of land that he was surveying. He walked briskly toward the spacecraft, and, as he cautiously approached the space disc, something very strange occurred. As he stood observing it from a safe distance, the hatch slowly opened, and what emerged was a silhouette of energy that had the appearance of a transparent haze. Jackson felt calm, as if time stood still, for what seemed like a significant amount of time. He knew this energy had come in peace and was able to communicate with his mind. With Jackson's permission, through telepathy, the energy requested to read every cell in Jackson's body. The alien energy field read his cells in a matter of seconds.

The alien energy could see all the futuristic designs of cars that Jackson had been drawing and creating. There was one car design; in particular, that Jackson had created to be very unique and unusual. The alien energy communicated why he had come to earth and informed Jackson that his car design originated from the powerful realm of Atlantis, and then showed him, in his mind, where the design originated. The alien energy communicated that he would meld with and occupy the disc, in its new form of the Astral Marten Space Car, into Jackson's favorite design. The car would be futuristic in outward and inward design. The alien energy confirmed the favorite model in Jackson's mind with the cells that stored this design within Jackson's vessel and mind, and asked permission, through contact with Jackson's mind, to transform the disc into the design of what would become the Astral Marten. Jackson silently gave his permission. The spaceship was then transformed into the futuristic car design, right there in the field of his parents' farm.

The reason the car was named "Astral Marten," was because the alien energy had a scheduled mission to make contact with the human, who was selected before he was born, to carry out the mission that was planned by the astral realm of Atlantis. It was also a cute sports car. In his design of the car on paper and in his mind, Jackson had obtained the designs by astral-projecting himself, as he entered other dimensions than our physical world, and this prepared him for contact that day, so he could assist in saving the human consciousness, within the basic realm of his own planet, through connecting the two realms back together again, through the strengthening of all minds.

The realm and beings of the civilization of Atlantis had explored all possibilities, and this was the best way, the only solution that they believed would work, to discover how to save the human consciousness and to reunite their advanced civilization with humans, the way it was, before the practices of the rulers of man erased the knowledge by covering over the code of freedom, and by siding with alien invaders for their own selfish purposes.

The beginning of the enslavement began with an alien invasion of evil beings, who were led by a group who had been cast out from their own civilization long ago, and who had a score to settle and an evil vendetta to satisfy, with the intention of supplanting our three cycles of consciousness (Bronze, Silver, and Golden Ages) with a fourth Age – the hard and rigid Iron Age, which caused a huge drop in the awareness and behavior of humans, so that they forgot how to live, and forgot that there existed any realm, except for our material one. Some humans, seeing that they could gain power by assisting the invaders, did so, which corruption was then recorded into the cells, creating a reality of darkness. Violence came after, which caused great pain and suffering to all humans, including the acts of engaging in wars, where humans killed one another. The actions of murder caused the once-pure spirits of humans to record violence in the cells of their vessels, both the cells of those who died and those who killed, which then shifted the codes of Earth away from Atlantis, causing them to no longer align, resulting in human spirits not being able to remain in the blissful realm.

This was how the separation of the two realms occurred, so very long ago. Human consciousness was separated by actions that caused knowledge of the realm of Atlantis to be erased from the cells of humans, while all minds were reprogrammed with dark experiences and realities. This situation, or new state of being, would not allow the spirit to return to the higher realm, upon death of the vessel, keeping all humans prisoners here and denying their advancement to the next level of reality. The system's purpose is to keep everyone in the false reality of chaos that prevents advancement of spirits to higher dimensions within the same planet, Earth, due to the enslavement within all societies of both rich and poor. Their own governments discovered the truth, realized the selfish benefits of enslaving the population, and have reimposed the consciousness-dropping practices, time after time, which they know will hold the spirits in this limited sustained reality, guaranteeing that they will return in the next cycle as slaves again. The timing of the soul's return to the pure dimension is a mystery to the creators of this reality overlay, and they do not understand it. By acts of violence, they kill the ones who threaten their schemes and plans, but those same individuals will return as many times as needed, picking up where they left off, and in each cycle attempt again to succeed in dismantling the enslavers' power over the population.

Jackson was in shock to learn what was conveyed to him in a brief moment, and he could not believe what his eyes had just witnessed and seen. Not only did a disc it safely land, but it also transformed itself into the futuristic, beautiful, gold car with a black, convertible top and white interior that he designed!

While the alien energy quickly communicated a small number of facts to Jackson, during the transformation from the space disc to the car, the engine was steadily singing quietly, and Jackson slowly approached the spaceship-now-automobile with great caution. First, he peered inside, through the side window, looking for the alien's energy, but, instead, he saw the dashboard of lights, that only he and Lady Jamis would ever see, and the transparent shifter, lit from within, that held within it the dimension of Atlantis, before it was erased from the memory of man. From there, he gazed between the bucket seats, and his eyes finally rested upon the slightly smoke-tinted windows. Jackson could feel the invitation to enter the already opened door. The alien said, "Enter the reality you know quite well." And so he did – with slight caution. Very slowly, he entered and slid into the fresh, cool, cushioned seats. Jackson felt a strong connection with the energy of the alien.

The alien conveyed to Jackson's mind, "I was your mentor on the other side, while you waited to be reborn here in this realm." At that moment, Jackson began slowly remembering his mentor, as he could feel the love the alien energy was emanating through the car. He knew this was a feeling he had not felt in a very long time, especially at such an intense level, or at least not that he could recall. It was at that moment that Jackson felt like his life finally had a great meaning and purpose. He now knew from where he had obtained all those car designs, images that were stored in numerous little cell pockets in his own energy and not in his vessel. The Astral Marten communicated with him by speaking to him telepathically, through his mind, feeding his cells with knowledge, so that he would regain the advanced knowledge he once knew, in a different life, a very long time ago, in the dimension of Atlantis' powerful reality.

It occurred to Jackson that he did not have much time to hide the car, as he was sure others might have seen the disc land to the ground. As he hurried to drive it toward the barn, the alien communicated, "Don't be concerned about my landing. I was invisible to all others. Only you alone could see me." He drove to where his workshop was located, and was able to hide the car for four years from his family.

One day, his brother Charles needed help on a project and stumbled upon Jackson, while he was sitting in the driver's seat of the Astral Marten, and he was positioned as if he had just been driving it. Charles was shocked to see such a vehicle, designed as the Astral Marten was. Charles asked his brother, "Jackson, where did you get this strange and very hip, car?" Jackson, caught by surprise, could only plead with his brother to not tell a soul about the strange car, and did not offer or disclose any information that would have compromised the mission of the alien car or the safety of his family. Instead, he gave Charles enough explanation to satisfy his curiosity. Charles promised to keep his big brother's creation a secret to only himself. He held his brother in very high regard and would never betray him.

Jackson is the one who left all the notes for Lady Jamis. In the notes, Jackson explained that the purpose of the vehicle was to gather data, so that the Universal beings could see the future of our actions and seek the knowledge that was needed, in order to help the humans connect their minds back to the powerful knowledge and dimension of Atlantis, by using their own free will.

The realm of Atlantis must be experienced and known, in this reality, before all spirits of human consciousness may unite back to the higher realm of reality. Atlantis must be successful, by returning the telepathic communication between the minds existing in the lived consciousness, and by acting as the command post, thereby serving a grand purpose to unite the two realities and reconnect all minds back to the original pure existence of love and the highest of all intelligence. Atlantis has been keeping close tabs on the progress of the strengthening of the human consciousness, knowing that our state of mind creates our vibration and, therefore, has everything to do with the required outcome. The desired results are increasing by the second, as the human consciousness expands toward the command post of Atlantis.

The rulers and their assistants, who have continued to practice and enforce the reality of enslavement, lack, and doom, tap and utilize the energy of each human, through means of inciting fear or greed (wealth, power, fame). This creates a false reality overlay by converting the enslaved humans' cells from once knowing, to being lost and separated from the powerful existence of Atlantis, our original gateway to our birth home connected to this reality. The continuance of the evil practices of the elites and rulers of this planet prolongs our stay here, and is an attempt to forever separate all spirits from their souls. It is the highest of military ranks, leaders of nations and their advisors, and some of the wealthiest, who also do drugs and drink occultic potions, for the purpose of staying in contact with the original invading aliens, the ones who changed our consciousness growth structure. It is the purpose of the rulers and elites (and their assistants) to make us weak by attacking us (with trauma situations), while we are unprepared to deal with their tactics, and then training us to expect – and even prefer – what they put into society for us to have or to want, causing us to divert our energy and resources into survival or greed, which prevents us from using our energy, time, and resources to examine reality and seek the truth. These tactics keep the knowledge under the radar, so that only the most intrepid ever find it. Without access to this knowledge, our minds are then open to their nefarious plans and actions, which they perpetrate by penetrating our minds to upload their programs of control and their lies about what is true and real, so as to mislead our powerful minds and incite us to commit acts that serve to perpetuate the separation of the realms.

Jackson explained, through his letters and notes, that all other humans could be influenced, because their minds were weak from the daily bombardment of the philosophies, the paradigms, the fear and greed inducing events and experiences, provided by the designers of this reality. These things keep people off balance, and thus, one or more steps behind the rulers and elites, making is less likely they will discover the truth. (Of course, their methods and technology have greatly increased in complexity and effectiveness since 1947).

To break through these effects and to discover the information that was needed, the car was to gather data – the words and ideas, stored as memories and those spoken, from the minds of humans it encountered, and also information that was stored in their cells, and it was to evaluate their individual vibration as words were spoken, so that the Atlanteans could do a complete data correlation, so that they could prepare the most effective plan to stop the ones who are the designers and facilitators of the false reality overlay from further affecting human consciousness, as well prevent any planetary destruction to Earth that would result from the evil ones' plans (including the twelve vortex explosions).

After the Marten delivered its gathered information to the Atlanteans in 1971, with Lady Jamis' help, it was time to connect all human minds of Earth with the knowledge of the superior law of Atlantis from the higher dimensions of reality. It was part of the rescue design to facilitate our learning of the concept of Science, so that we could be included, once more, with all others who adhere to the laws that govern all Universes and many dimensions of reality.

The universal beings of Atlantis are responsible for our energy and for the spiritual survival of all humans. Therefore, thousands of years ago, they provided knowledge that was to be for all, but, instead, the human leaders aligned with the invaders, who promised them riches and power, and they cooperated to create chaos to alter the human consciousness, by murdering and pushing others out of this realm. They then created societal cultures and religions to act as the so-called representatives of the higher realm, causing populations to worship gods, which practice has only served to be successful in keeping the populations divided and lost. Many wars have sprung up, as a result of religions, or the fuss over territories of solid ground. Many have been brainwashed into believing their fight is justified, never realizing how their minds have been trained to be limited in such a way that their capacity for thinking is stifled, which prevents them from being able to grasp the truth and evolve to a higher plain of existence, and thus, they commit acts of darkness. All actions based upon darkness, will be experienced in the near future, by all involved individuals, for all generations to come and societies will be composed of these individuals. Time will only yield chaos from yesterday's actions of darkness, that will then develop and increase for the near and far future – just as acts of love will yield greatness for the present and future to come. Each human exists in their own realm of creation. All the love you can give will yield in return more than you could ever imagine.

The command post represents the honor of worshiping the true source of our feminine energy, but the civilizations have been trained skillfully to promote darkness instead. This has been a repeated pattern of all the designers, through each and every cycle of consciousness. The Astral Marten was brought here to collect this data mentioned above, and it was no accident where it landed and who was to intercept it.

Jackson took many missions with the car, and traveled back to the dimension of Atlantis, the Universal dimension of reality, until his health deteriorated by old age, and he was no longer able to travel with the alien car and to transfer the data of his research. Jackson kept great records of the wars that transpired in his lifetime. He also had a close friend, who was very high in the military, who shared with him some of the senseless acts of the designers. Time passed, and Jackson died, leaving behind his two-year-old daughter, Samantha (Sam).

As Atlantis' informant, Jackson prepared to return to this physical realm for another tour within the false reality overlay in a new vessel, and waited for his proper time. The beings of Atlantis had to follow Universal laws and not interfere with free will, and they also needed a new candidate who was willing to carry on the space missions into other dimensions. Jackson would remain in the other realm, advancing his spiritual cells, while waiting to be rebirthed into the physical realm of man, to complete the mission for which he volunteered, to carry on the purpose of Atlantis.

It was not until 1969, when Sam, Jackson's sixteen-year-old daughter, was influenced by the same alien being (via the car, as it remained parked in the barn at her grandparents' old house), which communicated to Sam, during one of her visits to the property, that she suggest to her uncle and convince him, to start renting out her father's car. She did so, Charles agreed, and the next year, he placed it in his car lot. The last time Jackson had returned it to its command post, located in a dimension of the highest intelligence of Atlantis, the beings of Atlantis could see his health was not good, and they installed the microchip in the car, that acted as a GPS and a recording device, and to enhance the capabilities of the alien that existed in the car. From its vantage point of sitting in the car lot, which was situated by two very busy roads, as well from conversations in or near the car each time it was rented, the Astral Marten recorded a lot of needed data. The world will be briefed on what was recovered by, not only Jackson, but Lady Jamis as well.

Chapter 9

The Collected Data - What Does It Mean?

Lady Jamis enjoyed her visits to the dimensions of Atlantis' reality within the planet Earth. She was illuminated and saw how, before she had encountered the Astral Marten, she had been under a level of mind control by the designers of society, how they had been programming her since she was born, and how she listened to everything that was taught to her by her parents and teachers. She understood that the maintainers of the false paradigm suffered from the same mind control, because she had come to realize how the designers have had their plan in place for a very long time. She understood that people's actions follow from what they believe is true, and so these human maintainers are mind controlled stooges, misled to believe that power and wealth are all that matter. Lady Jamis gained such control over her mind that she could communicate telepathically with the divine beings of Atlantis.

The time has come to disclose all the data that has been collected from 1947 to the present, from high ranking government officials of intelligence agencies and the military to producers of culture by the way of movies and television programming to ordinary humans living their lives.

The programming of the minds of humans is a big deal to the above divisions of government. Limiting and controlling others is a wealth maker for the planners and their henchmen. The henchmen are lured into carrying out orders in exchange for promises of status, position, pleasure, or something of material gain. Sadly, these weak individuals have no idea what they are doing to themselves by strengthening the wrong side. Many will go through life thinking they have done great deeds, as far as public service, when all they have done is create more mess for others in the future to fix. The creators of the current existence depend greatly on helpers to keep the false program alive and well. These helpers will go through life thinking they have made a mark or an impact for themselves, by functioning as puppets. The sad fact is, all who are assisting the man-created, damning reality overlay, are putting effort into the wrong program. These lost spirits have no clue how to build an alliance with their own higher being, or higher reality. Time wasted, as a henchman in this reality leaves no room to prepare for when the cycle will end.

The cycle ending means a certain different way of thinking would have led to a reality of knowing the powerful emotion of LOVE, including knowing certain laws and facts that should have been understood and practiced while in this powerful consciousness. It's like graduation from school – it doesn't happen, unless you have passed your tests. When one passes the tests by obtaining and using the knowledge, the energy of spirit transitions from this reality to the higher reality, the one ending as the energy of the spirit exits and the new one beginning as that energy enters the reality of truth and purpose. Once the transition has completed, many are mortified by what they did or did not do, while in the false realm (here), when they were influenced by the tricks played by the ones who did not create the reality, but who certainly reinforced it through techniques. The act of murder is counter to the purpose of being here. Thievery, raping (for domination or to debase or exploit another person), power lust, hatred, and again murder – these are all acts that cancel access to the realm of love and harmony. The greatest purpose of each and every one of us is to grasp the message and take control of our own minds and build an alliance of cells from within our bodies and DNA.

Learn what is required – we all have one thing in common, and it is up to each person to protect the common interest, which is the human CONSCIOUSNESS. Not the planet, not our physical bodies, but the human consciousness. This is far more important than our bodies or any material item we create. Not even our status or position (that we believe we hold) means very little to what is important, if it does not serve a higher purpose, resulting in LOVE.

Lady Jamis and Jackson were aware of the facts related to this data, that the entire world was lied to and the truth withheld from the entire population. They knew that there was a separation from the other dimensions, realities, and planets, which only serves the purpose of preserving ignorance and limitation in the minds of the people alive in the physical consciousness. Our reality overlay creators needed the entire world to be enslaved via our minds, for the purpose of remaining in control of our minds, because our minds design and structure our realities, which, if we believe lies, leads to the control and enslaving of our spirits, forcing all of us to experience a very high level of chaos, some more than others.

Earth is not alone in space. Older Earth cultures depicted other beings in their art, and these beings are clearly not from Earth. Evidence is available for those who seek it and who will accept the truth, when they find it. Once the path widens and the spirit enters into a rest mode, it will carefully explore the truth. Facts will be gathered that will eventually lead to total freedom and understanding. The spirit of each human will awaken each day knowing knowledge, yet will have no recall of where it originated. The spirit will astral travel into other dimensions and absorb into their cells the path to love and freedom.

Jackson and Lady Jamis had learned this. If it had not been for their bravery, this information, which is about to be disclosed, may not ever have been delivered to the Atlantis dimension, and we would still be all blinded to the truth of what is real and what is coming to the Earth, that we would all be experiencing in the future, as a result of our enslavement and ignorance.

Through the data of the Astral Marten, we have learned that the designers of our culture and society created a space program, by using Nazi German intelligence, to place nuclear weapons in space, and that this is the foundation to their master plan for a one world takeover, which involves dominating the whole human consciousness. The divine beings of Atlantis will prevail in their purpose to return order back to the higher realm of reality. The men who seek to continue to perpetuate the enslavement of the human consciousness will be dismantled, one level at a time. The men who desire to continue the enslavement of the human consciousness have made numerous attempts to permanently sever our birth connection to the highest realm of reality, our original and perfect realm. They engage in the most horrific acts of violence that anyone could imagine.

When knowledge is purposely limited at numerous levels, it prevents the mind from seeking solitude to think. Instead, we seek distractions, so that we don't HAVE to spend time alone with our thoughts. Without the freedom of the mind, each person is doomed by what they think they are seeing, which is only a hologram of acts performed by darkness that is imposed upon us. These seem to be so real, but really they are illusions. There is no death of anything. It is a continued story, until the spirit returns here, to another physical body, in the next cycle.

As our minds have been manipulated, our experience of the dimension of Atlantis has been buried as an ancient memory, and is spoken of only as a fairy tale or myth. The existence of Atlantis is very much real, and they will someday return to our reality, after we strengthen our minds and remember we came here with a grand purpose – to learn and experience this part of existence in the material world. Each person must do their very best to learn the powerful Science by thinking. Thoughts lead to experiences and outcomes, both good and bad. The problem is, most people are thinking, seeing, and experiencing only the chaos of this reality, or only its materiality, which serves to sustain and hold each person from advancing toward a freedom of love and bliss. The greatest purpose of all is to connect our cells back to the codes of Universal laws and power of the mind. The methods of control did not previously allow this to happen, because it is the designers' plan to continue to hold all humans in this consciousness to this damned existence we have now. They don't want to let go of the false illusion of their creation – and their power.

Many people never consider the fact that time is running out for the planet, as the current cycle draws to a close, and we must greatly consider the danger of losing the opportunity to expand toward the truth, while strengthening our minds at the same time. If each human knew about the false programs of the illusory reality, then when a human died, where would their consciousness go? Would it return again to Earth, reborn in a new vessel? Surely, at some point, it must be discovered that each and every one of us came from, and will return to, another realm, both before and after each cycle. The nonsense that is learned here, which is called "education," has no connection to the realm from which we all originated. No amount of money, fame, or status will earn any one of us a spot in that blissful place. How we earn our way is through practicing, during our lives here, basic laws of Love, forgiving, and knowledge of the powerful mind.

The extensive details that were gathered by the Astral Marten, and delivered to the Atlanteans by Jackson and Lady Jamis, allowed them to discover the elements of purpose and how the environmental envelope for the growth of our human consciousness (the original cycles of Bronze, Silver, and Golden Ages) was deliberately altered to separate the knowledge from this mortal existence (by forceful overlay of the Iron Age cycle). One can only imagine the beings here at that time, who were here strictly on experiment with being physical beings, having freedom to live in harmony by following laws that prevented any chaos. Then, some lawless humans discovered how to change the reality and cause a separation from the realm of righteous laws (by the first murder). Murder created pain and suffering, an experience that created new emotions for them, that would also taint the birth code, further separating the two realms, forcing the being who died in the material to be rebirthed to the new mortal reality of enslavement. This was prior to the invasion from evil space beings, which only added to this problem. This information was learned from the data retrieved from the microchip in the car, which recorded directly into the alien's massive server within the Astral Marten. The governments still have not yet discovered how to travel through dimensions; they can only travel through orbit by spacecraft. They believe they are the most intelligent ones; not realizing their spirit is a space traveler with no limits, capable of visiting other dimensions and planets, while traveling through solid matter. Instead, they are trapped in this limited, corrupted, evil realm of man's creation.

The designers of this man-created realm are planning to make another, they hope "final," push for total takeover, and take all wealth and power from all civilians on this planet, while dismantling all religions at the same time (so that the state can be the people's god). This is why so many wars and genocides and massive deaths, caused by rulers of nations, have occurred in the past – to transfer wealth from the people to the rulers. Populations will continue to fall victim to these schemes, because there are certain elements of this reality that must be mastered while in this consciousness and state of being, *in large enough numbers*, before it can be stopped. Once you know the knowledge, it would not matter if your spirit were to be pushed out of this realm (that you died or where killed), because you would not return to further play your proscribed role in their wicked schemes.

Man worships material things. Their consciousness ambushed, then lowered by their own ignorance, humans focus on the comforts of life more than on the ability to love or the Science of creation, and so we continually fall short of learning the science of how to advance into other dimensions of reality. This has put people at risk to be trespassed, or even murdered, for their possessions, thereby preventing them from discovering the spiritual knowledge that is required before the cycle is up. The desire to have extreme material wealth is what creates and sustains their existence in ignorance and suffering, and causes them to claim this false reality as real and not master the science of creation – of how it is the mind that is responsible for all tangible items or actions we experience, and it is that mind that has the ability to advance to the next dimension of reality, by learning the alchemy connected to our existence, as it is the connection to the three cycles of the Bronze Age, the Silver Age, and the Golden Age, each of which harbors numerous levels of dimensions connected to Atlantis. Within these three cycles are advancement of complexity, depth, and understanding of all math and geometry. Our Universe holds many treasures in its massive data system, just waiting for us all to connect with it again.

Most of us have not made these discoveries, due to the system in which we live, the false reality, which reinforces itself, unless we break free, which begins with our noticing that things "aren't right," and then asking questions. Breaking free takes focus, determination, and great effort on the part of the individual. This system consists of the worship of material matter, false gods, and the false belief that one may own the elements of matter and energy, including humans. The elements exist for our experimentation only, not for ownership. When we learn how creation is conceived, it leads to both the invisible energy, as well as the visible, to become as one for us, creating what has been conceived in our mind, and which energy then commands the required elements to take a form, so as to deliver the powerful vibration, from the cells of the mind which is engaged by thoughts, to the visible world.

The steps of creation are amazing, when one fully comprehends how all things are infused by the power of thought, not merely by this realm alone, but by one of many realms and dimensions of Atlantis that are connected to our purpose and existence. Earth humans are capable of creation by their minds, just as all other creatures on Earth are to exist as a part of the beauty of the Earth, except that the animals do not have the capability that humans of Earth have, to create beyond their habitat.

There is one remaining place where Universal knowledge is stored, that is still available to humans-- the spiritual energy of their created DNA. Knowledge is power, but most of all, it is a gift, and has been within each human the entire time. From this science and knowledge will come the reward of wealth, which is more than mere money or material things (true wealth is knowledge and spiritual purity), and every human must own this knowledge and experience it, by bringing it back to life, as it is connected to superior law of all Universes.

The Starry Nebulas are where the human spirits of their souls re-enter this world, to re-experience consciousness. Babies are born every second around planet Earth, and this is how it happens. The nebulas birth a star for each spirited soul, and when stars "shoot" across the sky is when the spirit has completed its cycle-- that same star is returning to the source knowledge, carrying superior knowledge, or carrying ignorance of a man-created reality. When humans fail to achieve their birth knowledge of the wealth of the spirited soul, and not of material matter, or fail to discover it completely, they are sent back here after death, and reincarnate to Earth after a specific amount of time has passed, so that they can re-experience conditions that will allow them to learn what they failed to learn during the previous cycles of time. Eventually, due to many reincarnations, the planet becomes overpopulated, as it is right now. Too many are failing at succeeding, as the programs of man are constantly being cleverly designed to yield the outcome the designers planned out in advance, which entraps people in never-ending repeating cycles. The number of humans that succeed in locating their birth knowledge is minute, compared to what the number should be. Those beings of other dimensions within their planets have earned the advancement to achieve the knowledge that so many here fail to connect to.

From these teachings, we know that one must enter the next dimension of reality carrying the right spiritual knowledge, in order to reach Atlantis. Once one discovers, practices, and masters the levels of knowledge here discussed, one becomes a master in this consciousness state. When this is accomplished, one finally learns that Atlantis never disappeared. It is merely our ability to see that dimension that was erased, which happened when the consciousness shifted from awareness of knowledge to lack and fear. We must realize this discovery-- that Atlantis is still within our planet, unchanged, and that, when the separation of realms occurred, another dimension was created for us, to preserve Atlantis from the chaos in our own.

A great example of how our minds create our reality, is a person at their lowest point, such as being homeless – this is what extreme poverty is. Let's examine this carefully. The same homeless person has desired to change his or her circumstances by thinking and imagining a vision of another existence. The person begins to think on higher things, and as the thoughts take form, it begins to build the molecules within the cells of the body, and as the vibration occurs in a productive manner over time, the existence begins to improve the present reality. This is how the dimensions are experienced in the present consciousness. We are not required to die, before we can experience the other dimensions of reality. We can do this while we are still alive in this powerful consciousness. We have the power to advance right now and to connect to all dimensions of Atlantis, plus the original three cycles of consciousness for our planet, once it is felt and noticed that a change has occurred.

Each human must adhere to owning the ability of their mind and to utilizing their free will, as this guides the individual to connect to other realities of dimension, to master the laws of creation, and to not be any longer conditioned by the controllers of society, especially by the reality of war, which creates and feeds fear. We need to understand that all humans consist of two realities – one is visible and the other is invisible. This means the vessel is the visible and the spirit is the invisible. Our lack has erased our ability to see the great city of Atlantis and both visible and invisible are connected to the superior law of higher dimensions, which reigns over the feminine and her Universe.

The laws that are in place in this current reality are meant to create confusion and fear. But, once it is understood that fear is the cause of enslavement, and how our own energy is used against us, to sustain this current man-created reality, this can be reversed. The energy of our fear is very damning to us all. Our energy is used against us, to keep all humans weak and easy to control. And, it works! Look around yourself and notice what happens over the entire world and what actions are being imposed on humans against their will.

Once we understand the powers of our soul's energy and the power of the Free Will, we shall not be enslaved by our same species any longer. Knowledge and ignorance are both stored in the cells in the vessel. One is man-created and the other is a natural superior knowledge that is connected to the higher realm of numerous dimensions and superior realities of knowledge.

Within each cell in our body are programs of one of these two realities. How we have been taught to think, act, or exist is not by the design of the higher dimension of Atlantis, but by man – by greedy and very corrupt men and women. When the correct knowledge is not present within the cells in our vessel, we are at their mercy and only react to the design provided for us by society, which dictates improper programming to our cells, which creates a programmed reaction and sustains our current reality of doom, which is why WAR (and contentions of all kinds, including riots) has such purpose in their plan. War presents such extreme trauma to people, that it acts as a preventative to our finally learning the truth, and is just a bad trick that was created long ago that has kept us apart from the truth.

Once the mind has been infused with stealth superior knowledge, the cells will fire up and began to convert to the correct program of superior knowledge. The ability of our mind to send signals of desire and for the invisible realm of Atlantis to react, is the most powerful way to deliver what we are requesting. The reason so many people have yet to discover this, is due to the havoc that is planted in us, which creates cells that consume the entire body, before it is discovered that the body is reacting to the reality of the cells that are within the vessel.

The Astral Marten was able to determine how human rulers were enslaving their own species – and they did it by creating their own version of what they desired and imposed their version on everyone else – by not following the superior rule of Universal laws that govern all Universes.

The designers realized that, even after the reality hijack, the necessary knowledge would still be available to the masses of humans, because it could come from space, and they wanted to prevent that, so they created a program that they intended would act as a shield, a barrier, to prevent anyone, including our transiting spirits, from entering this atmosphere or even from exiting (as upon death of the vessel), thus trapping human spirits. What these rulers did not comprehend, nor did they anticipate, is that energy is energy, no matter what it is, and although material matter may not enter, the energy of the soul, which is the spirit, is also energy, like the shield, and has the powerful ability to overcome being destroyed by the barrier, because it is undetected by the barrier. The spirit energy blends in, as though it was identical to the energy of the barrier, creating oneness, and thus can penetrate the barrier. The same action would apply to spirit beings, who may come to help us, and who would arrive here and need to pass the barrier in ships of energy, to reach us. Information is also energy, and it can pass the barrier, also.

It was foolish of the designers of the false reality and of the energy barrier not to realize that there is nothing they could possibly do to stop the shift in awareness from happening. Their total addiction to power over others has so corrupted their thinking that they thought they could control this, too.

Our knowing of this knowledge gives us the resource that is understanding what has been done and what will fix the wrong programs that the body has in each cell. The wrong programs in each body cell create numerous realities – mainly fear, lack and doom – and these stifle us from experiencing other higher dimensions of reality, while we are alive in this powerful realm and existence. Once the cells of all humans have been replaced with source superior knowledge, the entire planet will exist in harmony and peace.

The Atlantean microchip enabled the Astral Marten to seek out the methods and organization of the societal design, as well as the individual designers who were responsible. The car was designed to decode the DNA by signaling a vibration to all the humans who sat in the car or who were within range of its computer scanners, from all walks of life. The car was capable of decoding the cells in each human's body, in order to make known to the Universal beings what the correct knowledge is that must replace the bad cells. These bad cells must be eliminated and replaced with what is real, which is superior knowledge from the higher realm of all dimensions.

This is achieved by thinking and by building the intellect up. If we are not thinking, we are not expanding our minds. We are in neutral gear. When this occurs, the system controls us and stifles our abilities to advance. Just imagine – no reality of war. Imagine – all serenity and love around the planet, while all beings are building knowledge. Imagine – a unity around the world without religions, but mirrored spirituality of unity. Imagine – a world of complete love and peace. This includes all of humanity.

The invaders continue to reproduce realities by building their own alliance of chaos. It is what they do, and is all they know how to do.

This car was sent from Atlantis and was beyond any technology from our planet Earth. It could analyze the health status of a human, as it did with Jackson. It could x-ray, scan for all the drugs that were in the body, and identify what the constraints were, which were preventing the mind of that individual from seeking a higher existence. It could also determine why the chemicals had been taken – usually from emotional pain or from boredom, but also from willful immaturity and thrill-seeking. The Astral Marten was able to determine that the compromised health of many was due to the wrong programming of the mind, that created cells to vibrate at a level of lack, fear, and doom. This caused the immune system to weaken and to not have the strength or ability to keep the vessel and its organs healthy. The car had the ability to monitor all energy, energy patterns, and activity of past and future events, as a time traveler, just as John Titor, a name without a face, time traveled from the future, but from a more advanced civilization. This information is very much real, as the false system of Earth was carefully designed to prevent society from learning this ability, too. It is a great purpose, to balance the energy of this planet, once and for all.

The Astral Marten also retrieved data from far back in time, from when the invasion from space occurred, before the time of the Egyptians. The computers captured past thoughts belonging to ancestors, which are the reincarnated Earth beings of the present time, in the right now. It was able to read thoughts from the past, because it mattered not how far back a thought had been created or conceived. It was determined that all thoughts will exist in the atmosphere of a planet for eternity. They will always remain, endlessly awaiting to reunite with the consciousness of the mind who created it. Only when the mind has the ability to be open to knowledge, will the existing thoughts from the past be drawn to the mind that is pulling towards them, from its own desire and vibration to exist in the highest of all plains, as thoughts are drawn to the magnetic force of the mind. Of course, this works not only with the positive experiences and thoughts of the far past, but also with the negative ones.

The Astral Marten also retrieved data that consisted of the thoughts from elsewhere in the cosmos, and which also came from other dimensions of reality within this Universe. These formed a shared network, communicating telepathically with each other, by the consciousnesses existing in all Universes. How this knowledge came to be in our atmosphere was due to the ability of the energy of our minds to signal and travel to other far distant planets and dimensions. All thoughts are, therefore, local thoughts! The program of the false reality has limited the minds of humans and has forced some humans to astral travel, and so they become time travelers, in order to seek the truth of their abilities to connect to other dimensions of realities in the vast Universes.

The Astral Marten also discovered that every war that ever was fought was the very same program, merely repeated, and that war, as a concept and a memory, previously existed as thoughts and actions millennia ago, having become an entrenched, permanent program in both the body and the mind of the human race from just one occurrence in the past.

These very same, ancient programs would be continued by the invading rulers of the past, the same ones who imposed the Iron Age upon us today, in order to keep humans enslaved, by taking advantage of these ancient programs existing in each cell. Our vessels have been harboring these programs on a cellular level, ever since the original, superior knowledge was stolen and buried, deep within depths of our spirits, and then slept, along with our memories of Atlantis, where it remains separated from the oppressed soul. The souls would be able to experience freedom only when the vessels, along with all of man's programs that rested with the vessel, are dismantled for eternity. The spirit would visit all sorts of places within other dimensions, depending upon their beliefs and focus, while trying to make it back to the harmonious reality of Atlantis − the city of love, knowledge, and creation, of what the mind created, a grand city as our home base of knowledge.

Our ability to communicate telepathically with the Atlanteans was also disconnected in the distant past, because of the separation of realms. That time was also when the vessel became a prison for the spirit, with terms of years determined by matching the length of the life cycle. Over time, the layers of illusions grew thicker and thicker, by adding more confusion to the reality of each spirit and collectively, until the spirit finally buried it completely, although some spirits continue to seek the sheltered realm of Atlantis, primarily by astral meditation and meditation. As morning arrived, the spirit would return from other realms, and once again occupy the vessel, until the next session of rest was at hand for the vessel.

No matter what schedule the vessel was on, the Astral Marten was able to understand the design, and the confusion, and how the reality must switch from the spirit taking the back seat to being the pilot and the compass, to lead by its communication with its own command post, the dimension of our Universe, and not of the ego and personality, as both of these are ignorant to the real facts.

The data proves that all the wars were created in order to prevent the spirits of the humans, who willfully engage in the act of taking of the life of another human, from returning to its home dimension, condemning it to reincarnate, until it learned the ways of love. Without realizing what they are doing to themselves, the human henchmen in wars seal their own fate by their acts of ignorance. The Atlanteans placed sanctions against all violators of cosmic laws, including what they did and continue to do to cause and support the spiritual and material enslavement of their fellow humans. The purposes of the imposed false reality overlay were and are to gain and maintain complete and total power over populations and line the pockets of the rulers, including their human helpers and maintainers, who were and are given incentives for their cooperation. Their actions will guarantee a repeat to this realm for themselves, where they will remain spiritually enslaved, with the illusion of money and wealth as their highest reality, creating for them a blind spot, behind which hides the superior knowledge – for these and for all whom they enslaved. This created a reality of debt for most, convincing people to "keep up with the Joneses," as they try to outdo each other. These have been simple tactics, which have effectively controlled the entire population, and supported the main agenda, which is to cause and ensure that spirits will return to this realm of existence and be reborn, after each life cycle is over, to be re-enslaved again. All who fail to learn what is required allow the reality planners to depend upon a huge number of enslaved people to be there, so that they can build their wealth and power structures in every generation.

Thanks to the Astral Marten, the data has been gathered to find the most practical way to return back control of a human's mind to them, and that is by activating the free will, that is to think with a clear consciousness. What the Universal beings mean by that is, to realize that all the creation of debt, property taxes, anything that weighs the mind down, is not real, never has been, and never will be – in other words, to see through the illusion.

This planet cannot ever be purchased, as our energy will always exist and the Earth provides to us our ability to exist. It is therefore false for any one person to think they will own anything that has been only loaned to them, including a physical body, while each life span of cycles exist at different intervals of life, however long it may last. When our vessel dies, we shall be able to take with us only the superior knowledge of the dimensions we are reconnecting to, that which is required of us to learn while we are here. We will not take with us, when our vessel dies, anything that was of material creation. We will be able to take only the methods of our ability, of how we created and experienced the material object. No object should ever be placed before the laws of love to others. Once a thought has been conceived, no matter what it is, in time, it will become our reality. It will remain to exist for eternity, and can be drawn to us in our next cycle by the desire of the creator of that thought. When this happens, we are usually unaware that it is a repeated thought from another time, in the past. The desire, vibration, and will are what draws to the mind the very same experience or desire. Thoughts of thousands of years ago will still exist, as the energy sustains our every thought. As long as we exemplify the vibration of that thought, it will be drawn to us.

The divine Beings desire us to know and understand that the Universe belongs to not one single person, and therefore it cannot be rented, taxed, or sold. The material matter is provided by the Earth, for all to live, to share, to learn, and to exist as one, in a reality of equality for all. It is not so that some may be excluded from what the planet has offered all – a place to eat, sleep, and drink.

The only thing that is prohibiting many from discovering and experiencing the true knowledge is that the minds of the spirit have not yet experienced the freedom of the other dimensions of reality. We all have the ability to connect to these other dimensions, through our minds and our actions. The method can be achieved by first denouncing the illusion of man's practices and ignorance, which illusion neutralizes the mind with realities of limitations. Then, we must realize that each and every one of us have had the power to rise above the illusion of limitation the whole time. The time has come to realize that we are here for a purpose, and are not here to be enslaved any longer, by our same species of humans, who, by honoring a phantom god, or a particular man, who may be acting as a leader, seems to do very little for the poor and meek, but who seems to continually bless the wealthy. This is a great clue as to who is doing all the thinking and who is taking action! The human mind creates all there is to experience. It is not magic tricks, just great Science and spirit.

Chapter 10

An Explanation of Pyramids

Lady Jamis found her purpose in this life and stepped into the unknown, when she sat in the Astral Marten. She discovered that its energy was far more intelligent than the structure it was dwelling in (the body of the car). Lady Jamis traveled very far, to carry out what Jackson did not get to see to completion in the previous cycle. The results of this mission would make available to more people the knowledge to continue on this journey of freedom and Unity.

The remedy required to restore this great consciousness back to its original existence is rapidly approaching us all. Jamis was able to deliver the greatest amount of data to the dimension of Atlantis, so as to save planet Earth and the spirits, longing to return to their souls, which still reside in the dimension where they originated long ago, which also currently exist in Earth's atmosphere.

The Universal being from Atlantis, who exists as a form of energy within the Astral Marten, communicated to this lady, "Only when you open your heart to the love that has been waiting for you in the Universe – only then will you understand the true meaning of life and living." Lady Jamis realized, at that moment, how every human on Earth would kill or cut a throat, to have money or to pay off debt, or even forsake another to have the finer things in life, and that these things really enslaved, not only her, but all others as well. She learned how consciousness would always be a constant, and that it is just a transition of change and form. There is no end to time – it too, is a constant existence. She could not believe how intelligent these beings of Atlantis were, and how everything is so obvious, if one would just stop and consider what is being conveyed: consciousness is what counts and matters and affects us all. We must strengthen the mind in order to save our own consciousness. Consciousness will always be constant, and the consciousness can only be experienced while in the physical plane. Experiences of what is incorrect will only repeat the wrong recordings that have been taught, ever since the beginning of our knowledge and love, which was replaced with fear.

This was hard to imagine, at first, but as Lady Jamis was shown the data, she knew every bit to be true, and she was determined to share what she discovered with the Universal beings who had provided her with intelligence beyond what she already knew, which was nothing, as compared to what was shown to her after she communicated with them in the dimension of Atlantis.

Lady Jamis was informed of others on Earth, who have been working with the Universal beings to bring enlightenment to all, in order to save the human consciousness, which is trapped in a third dimension reality, here on planet Earth. One of many beings, who are doing their very best to act as the light of love of the Messiah, who once walked among men, is one lady in particular. She was instructed to create a special pyramid, the Pyramid of Love and Gratitude, that harbors great powers within its purpose. The instructions to create it originated from a powerful dimension of the feminine realm, and the pyramid would exist as a reminder of the great power of all minds – a symbol of the freedom of the mind, and that the Universe is one, with all dimensions of a superior realm connected to each other by the power of LOVE.

The pyramid is a symbol that acts as a reminder of the intelligent beings we are, because our gift of knowledge is from a higher realm of reality. The Universal beings transported most all humans here, to Earth, from very ancient times, as far back as when the Atlanteans were still a part of our once more-powerful consciousness. The power and energy of the pyramid that this other lady made is now a part of this reality – it was created into a 3-D form years ago. As a powerful symbol, it assists us, by offering us the truth, so that our shift of the consciousness may finally return, so we can escape from enslavement to illumination, with the reality of LOVE and GRATITUDE.

It was decided by those who guided her, even before the pyramid was made into physical form, that the moment it came into this realm of existence, within this level of consciousness, its purpose became a part of our mission to break away from the created reality. The thought that created it became a permanent fixture of our reality, even though the thought originated from another dimension. The purpose of the pyramid will be for eternity in this consciousness. The pyramid's energy or knowledge can never be destroyed. Destroying the pyramid's physical form would not erase the invisible energy of its own alchemy – to exist as energy in matter, which reminds all of their birth right; nor would that act delete its purpose – its purpose will exist for eternity.

The pyramids of Giza are a mirror of Orion's Belt, a reminder of the one who designed them, and why. Their intended purpose was to create a separation from our celestial home. The secret code of the pyramids of Giza is known by high ranking officials. The reason for having three pyramids, is that each one represents one of the three cycles of consciousness, which are the Bronze Age, the Silver Age, and the Golden Age. Those pyramids are constructed with four sides, so the purpose is to create a fourth reality, which is the Iron Age of Man, causing man to turn his back on the celestial realm, from which we all originated. The pyramids harbor their own auras in color within the laws of Alchemy: red, blue, and green. This is the power of our consciousness and of each cycle of the three key growth cycles of our consciousness, mentioned above.

The Astral Marten has successfully put the puzzle of the past back together, so that we all can rise above the sanctions placed against us by our own ignorance. There is no man, woman, or child, who is better than the next. Their level of education in this world is what determines their value to the current system. It seems that man's reality offers many rewards for being a great team player and participating in all of the schemes of distraction from our true purpose that have been created. What man has failed to do, is to tell the truth of what you just read. The truth is that none of us originated from here.

There is no time like the present to start awakening the codes connected to Orion's Belt and seek the truth. This is our golden opportunity to experience true freedom of the mind, of really having the experience to be free to think and know. Even if we cannot see the truth at first glance, it is there. It always has been there, the whole time – the ability of the mind to connect to other realms of thousands of planets and all dimensions of reality. We have had the ability to re-experience this realm through other dimensions of reality, while we are alive and in the physical cloak of matter, which is the body, the vessel. All of this information has been within the spirits of all humans, the entire time.

Chapter 11

Jamis in the Other Dimension
– An Awakening of Cells

While Jamis and her unborn child were in the other dimension, they had two very unique experiences. The first happened while the Astral Marten's data was being retrieved from the alien's energy and data server. While the data was being uploaded, she had time to explore this other dimension. Jamis was invited to take a bike ride on a long desert road that had miles of pure white sand on both sides of a long stretch of pavement. She started out on her journey, on this weightless bicycle, but she was not expecting what was about to happen. The vehicles in this other dimension were very small, but very fast, and as she was riding along with the flow of traffic on the white bicycle, that had wide red rubber tires, something bizarre happened. There was a patch of tiny pebbles across the entire stretch of the road, and all of a sudden, the cars began spinning out of control. Jamis lost her balance and, in slow motion, fell over while a puff of air gently delivered her safely onto the soft, fine, white sandy shoulder of the desert road. Jamis' unborn infant was giggling inside of the womb! Jamis could actually hear her daughter laughing at the cars through her mind. Each time she attempted to get up, the cars were still spinning out of control all around her, but strangely, they were not crashing into each other.

It was as if the cars and the occupants were being playful with the baby. Finally, two cars quickly raced up, stopping immediately in front of Jamis, giving her time to get up and to safely move herself further off the side of the road. She hurried and pulled the bike safely away from the bike travel lane.

Jamis was then about to get back up on the bike, but as she looked over her shoulder, she saw that coming directly toward her from behind was a huge dump truck that appeared to have also lost control. In that same moment, her daughter said from within her womb (and to her mommy's mind), "Mommy look, look a big old truck." The truck was heading right toward her, even though she was on the side of the road. She froze, and knew it was going to run her and the unborn baby over. Then, all of sudden, at the last second, the dump truck began to propel itself and became airborne. As it was flying over Jamis' head, she calmly laid down on her back and watched it, and, as it flew over her, she saw the underside of the dump truck. She counted five axles, while the wheels were still spinning in the air. The truck landed just on the other side of where she was lying. After the truck touched down, Jamis hurried, got up, safely climbed on the bike, and headed back to where the Astral Marten was being decoded by the Atlanteans. It was time to return to the dimension of the Earth she knew – the one that had been damned.

Upon her return, Lady Jamis considered in great detail the false reality that the designers created long ago – a reality of fear and hopelessness – forcing many to settle for the reality, as the cells from within them validated the lack that was without. She could see how this plan will soon be dismantled, and not those who were the original creators, but their facilitators, old and new, the ones who have continued to create more scenarios, will also discover their superior purpose. What they had not considered was that the Earth beings have the power to no longer be programmed by all their tactics of fear and death, that their power is not permanent.

A great example of this reality programming for confusion is the programming of subliminal suggestion by public broadcasting of news and entertainment media. The experience was originally made available to us, with the intention to improve our knowledge, but it was co-opted for the nefarious plan, to plant life-draining and energy-draining thoughts in all minds, thoughts that caused automatic thinking, under the radar, and promoted control, in any way the facilitators desired. It was successful, so these tactics were added to movies (including DVDs), also.

The wars that have been conducted are the greatest application of this programming, because the rulers get the people to 'buy in' to the idea of war and favor the idea. This is old knowledge – staging an event, so as to present an act of war, so that the people give their consent for the war, which then leads to murder. No matter how any one of these civilizations proclaims their justice for attacking others, it is still murder – the worst act of humankind, besides the rape of a child, including both females and males. These practices create trauma, which closes the mind off from the powerful spirit. All must rise above these experiences, and also the practices perpetrated upon us of subtle mental manipulation, done for the purpose of secretly obtaining our "consent," and plant seeds of doom, such as experiences of fear of the destruction of our consciousness, especially in torn, dismantled countries, such as many in Africa, Cuba, India, parts of the Middle East, and everywhere war or government mass killings of their own people have taken place. The illusion that there exist financial concepts (money and financial wealth) has deceived people into believing that money matters, and this is believable, because when companies or whole economies fail, this leads to lack among the people, which leads to famine and despair, and then people to just fail at life in general.

When one becomes aware, one can then identify what has been shown and how it is intended to make everyone who witnesses the same thing create the absolute wrong information in their cells that will become the reality of their existence. This is what Lady Jamis realized, and this is what many others will soon realize. The power of us all is in how we think, act, and exist. The emotion of love will change the mindset of the powerful spirits, and they will see more clearly what has been truly going on, how our way of existing was well planned out, very carefully. But, we can do something about it. All it requires is an open mind to think rationally about what has been happening in the current cycle of each individual's life, at least for himself or herself.

Considering that, once that entire burden is released, what will the mind do now? That is easy – it will think! And thinking invokes imagining, which leads to creating, and creating brings an action that leads to results, and soon we will understand the level of control we have had the entire time. Thinking is what connects us to other dimensions; we can't experience them unless we have the ability to use our heart for love and the mind to make the connection.

The reality of our planet was not supposed to be as it has been, and the time has come to educate all on the basics and how everything is based on love. This story has been written, in order to invoke the senses of the mind to awaken the encrypted code within the DNA. The other dimensions are absolutely real, and my cells recorded the details accurately, so that this incredible story could be used as a tool to awaken the seekers that love a great, fascinating sci-fi story. The car was deliberately sent to Earth as a powerful high-tech computer, that was a real energy that became disguised as a car, even though it really was an energy from another dimension that converted from a spacecraft to a stealth, muscle car. The car's mission was to seek out and to master the design of society and reality that had been created by man to enslave the spirits by keeping all stumped, so as to continue the program of enslavement from generation to generation in this – the most powerful realm of all dimensions.

The Astral Marten was designed to succeed in its mission, because all other Universes are dependent on the survival of our species. If we fail, it reflects on their success to save us from the enslavement of man, and, since the enslavers of men have intended to eliminate our guardians, as well, they have a personal stake in the success of the mission.

Earth is, and always has been, the planet of enlightenment, created outside of the perfect realm to make possible the experience of the emotion of love, the highest vibration the Universes could ever experience. It was the human race that held the key, who would expose their love to the vast universes, universes that were counting on this energy to survive. The Astral Marten's realm of dimension was slowly dying, unless the humans were able to use their powers and abilities to love. Instead, man has held the enlightened planet down, oppressed it in ways that were specifically engineered to prevent the love that is required and needed to save so many planets. So much will be lost, if this is not corrected immediately. The humans must know, they must be informed, that once all other Universes are gone, their very own universe will not be able to sustain the sorrow that will result, and her solar system will pull apart, because the Universes won't be there to hold her Universe in place, so all of creation will come to nothing, especially the precious creation of humans, with demigod-like abilities, that were designed to provide love to the other Universes. It was our purpose to share the blueprint of our unique design, and our realm was to be the darling of all dimensions of realities. The dream was lost the moment our spirits became enslaved and were held down in a realm based on matter, material that would not exist if it were not for the powerful mind.

Humans! Please wake up before it is too late! Realize that you hold the key to life, love, and eternity, to all other dimensions of realities in our Universes. Please locate your hidden powers that have been within you the entire time. Use your powerful free will and make a choice. It has always been within you, everyone, and it has been that simple – a choice to decide to think for yourself and not be controlled by the very same species that had no hand in creating you, but has only programmed you with the incorrect information, and that has lied to us all, and made us feel inferior to the illusions of their program. If not corrected very soon, all Universes will lose in this, including the one containing planet Earth, which is Atlantis.

What also has been hidden from the humans is the fact that, before the invasion, all planets in our Solar system were in closer proximity to each other. Planet Earth held the full house of the zodiac, because it can only be seen from the perspective of being on our planet. All beings on the nearby planets were to achieve the opportunity to advance to planet Earth, so they could master the final levels of power. The twelve, monthly, Zodiac symbols are the power and creation of the feminine realm. The design of the constellations was meant for her superior knowledge to be mastered by all beings from other planets that travel in, who arrive here in the very same way as Earth beings travel, by energy (spirits can go through the shield). All planets were placed in the correct order, and the one planet that held all the Knowledge was and still is Earth, which exists with more dimensions of reality than can be experienced, while we are alive in the flesh. Glimpses of these other dimensions can be had, while in this realm, but the experience of them exists outside of this realm. The Universe barely shadowed the planet and each Zodiac within the second largest constellation, which is the Virgin symbol, was illuminated in a white glow of light, that could be seen from as far away as one could imagine, and which announced to all Universes its grand power and knowledge, as all dimensions that are connected to the constellations will be experienced once again – the multiple wonders of all Universes.

Chapter 12

Surprising, How Things Turned Out

The clock is ticking. Please be reminded to gain the correct superior knowledge that is already blueprinted into your DNA that scientists have referred to as "Junk DNA." They have yet to explain it, because it is of Universal knowledge and is the birthright of each inalienable human, who did not originate from this planet called Earth. It is the Free Will that activates the DNA of neurons and molecules within the cells. They are to become pro-active and delete the programs and systems man has created. Once this happens, the ability to use all senses, along with the abundance of Universal powers, will finally be discovered, and will then come to life. The moment this occurs for all humans, all Universes will also be united and saved, because in the highest creation of all dimensions, humans will finally understand that the mind is what connects us to all other dimensions of reality.

We have been trained to depend on the sight of the eyes, in order to confirm if something exists or is real. This type of thinking and practice limits our ability to connect to these other dimensions – telepathically, like we once did. If we can't experience these dimensions by our vibration, then it is a fact that our cells are pre-programmed to be drawn into the numerous false paradigms of man's ill intent to enslave the spirit to a realm that has no purpose to any other– a false reality of darkness. Multiple dimensions are connected to the energy of the creator. All is created from the desire of all humans and their very powerful minds.

Objects exist in this realm, but we cannot see them, due to our lack of knowing, which holds back our ability to discover what is required of us all. There is so much knowledge available to all who desire to seek a way out of what we all have been tricked into believing until now. The experience of the Astral Marten allowed Jamis to see the past, present, and future with great clarity. The vision and experience of the old frame house, while she was driving the stealth, space vehicle. She never saw the house while driving her own personal vehicle. With the car's help, she peeled off the layers of deception, which had transpired over time with each cycle of life she lived either as a male or, as now, a female. Each time she entered the spacecraft, with its resident alien energy, she went deeper and further into all aspects of her own cycles, which experience was created by the powerful dimension of Atlantis. With the help of this energy, Jamis was then able to see into other dimensions. We have been trained to think that Atlantis simply disappeared, while the whole time it has been there all along, here in a physical realm, just hidden from us, because of our lack of knowledge to see beyond this sustained reality, which is the false reality overlay. The energy of the Astral Marten originated from the civilization of Atlantis. It left its powerful realm, in order to enter this damning realm of enslavement, slipping under the radar of detection of man's technology, to awaken the ones trapped in this false paradigm of reality (that man has created out of ignorance), by reuniting with the pupil (Jackson) it once mentored in the other realm.

The system of man is finally being dismantled and is failing by the minute. The signs are in plain sight! Only if one would not panic and use their mind more productively, the ones who further self-engineered this system of practice, that has stifled all of humanity from their purpose, will eventually fail. There absolutely is nothing they can do to stop the other dimensions from taking back their rightful position in this consciousness, from retrieving the energy of spirits from the unknowing thieves, who ignorantly continued to denounce the higher dimensions, which are connected to the feminine energy of our creation and of this planet. We all stand to benefit from learning about our own capable powers, that the mind has the ability to reunite us all to these other dimensions, which are connected to the natural three cycles of consciousness.

We shall not allow any further, the tactics used by government to continue this control of our consciousness, attempting to erase our eternal energy of love – it is obvious to see that it will not ever be destroyed, but where our energy lives, and under what conditions, depends upon our knowing or not knowing. The status of our not knowing our knowledge permeates the current sustained reality, but this is not our intended realm and never will be. You must understand and accept this true scientific fact. Only discovering the Knowledge for yourself will change your status of whether you live inside or outside of this false reality.

The previous journeys of the Astral Marten secured the success of our planet. It traveled so far, through numerous dimensions of reality, to return to its own powerful realm, and succeeded in returning the numerous dimensions of reality back to all spirits of earth. This became possible, all because Lady Jamis and Jackson became as one, as Lady Jamis learned that the child in her womb is Jackson reincarnated. This part of knowledge was to show everyone that our energy is a blend of both male and female. That each gender can return as the opposite of what it was in the previous cycle.

The next phase of discovery will be handed to the next traveler once she is physically old enough. Lady Jamis gave birth to the returning spirit of Jackson, now a beautiful baby girl, whom she named Harmony of Atlantis. The child has a great understanding of both realms and how she would lead the entire population back to its original existence, the one from before the separation occurred in very ancient times. Harmony's numerous missions with her mother will bring great discovery, to help us learn how to expand our minds beyond the limited reality of man, so that together we can grow and overcome the system that serves to only enslave and holds us to this artificial realm of existence.

We have a precious gift called life. Within the cycle of life we have consciousness and a grand purpose.

It is in our best interest to learn what is, not only required, but real. The consciousness we are gifted to experience must be honored and protected. The lesson upon death is where all the knowledge has been held. We must learn our powerful knowledge before the cycle ends and before the transition of death occurs.

Harmony developed skills of walking and talking much earlier than the average infant. The reason this occurred was that her cells were filled with Jackson's knowledge and discovery after his encounter and journeys with the alien energy that occupied the space vehicle, and who was his mentor from the other side. Harmony also absorbed all of her mother's knowledge, while she was in the womb. Because this child had no experience to recall of man's reality lurking in her cells, this child was pure and powerful! She will carry on the purpose of her past experienced cycles with the Astral Marten, the alien mentor. Her cells of knowledge will not allow her to be subjected to the seedy environment that other beings have had to overcome, including remaining trapped for many life cycles. Harmony will never experience the old, false realm of reality, because Harmony's cell base is only connected to Atlantis' realm of existing. Harmony will cause the consciousness of humans to shift back to the reality of Atlantis. The reality is in the process of the transition right now. Many political criminals will be exposed for what they are and how they have existed, as lost misguided spirits who were set up to fail and who fell. These criminals are hiding within the governments of all countries on planet Earth. The individuals who are the facilitators of this chaos will be given a chance to repent of their crimes and save their own consciousnesses, before their cycle ends. The criminals are still treated with respect by the Atlanteans. Their Free Will is protected, honored, and respected.

The next phase of existence will have no governments or laws of man existing any longer. The beings of Earth will not recall the ordeal they had experienced of all the crimes of lack and passion, while trapped in this realm of man. They will return to their powerful minds of love, peace, and oneness. They will not have any recordings of all the wars, murdering, and separation of the two realms. All religions will be erased from their cells and they will all see each other as energies of love. There will be no cultural acknowledgment of one person being superior to the other. All beings will gradually gravitate toward the shift in consciousness, and will take back their powerful minds and the experience of pure love once again, no longer craving materialism or the desire to own any item connected to the elements of this planet, not even the physical human. The cycle will end, and the beings will have succeeded in fulfilling their purpose of being here. The beings will have discovered that the elements of this realm were merely an experiment that turned out to be a dangerous lesson for all. It has been a very, very, long time since the two realms were joined as one. In this realm it seems like it has been forever, but in the realm of Atlantis, it has been only a short time. Gaining awakened minds with the hearts filled with love and Harmony, is our greatest purpose. We are energy of oneness, and no physical shell or a reality of darkness shall ever divide us ever again.

Harmony has telepathically communicated a very important message! "Help yourself by seeking the true answers before your cycle ends. Don't chance it, and dismiss what the Astral Marten has successfully done. Learn something superior to what man has taught you. Study well, and master all you can. Carry something with you that will impact the other realm – carry back to that realm of origination, that has been so patiently awaiting a return by all human spirits, while knowing the great powers of love and knowledge from all the great experiences they discovered, while they were alive in their cycle, in the flesh. The world has fallen apart, both politically and socially, as part of the plan to point all in the correct direction. Once it is understood by us all that we create by thought and that we make reality exist by the amount of love we have to give and are willing to receive, many will lose their power and control over this realm.

The journey of the Astral Marten has proven to be worth the effort to save as many spirits as possible. All the customers who rented this car were aided to help themselves to think higher thoughts, as the car made a lasting impression on all who experienced this space cruiser. The ones who drove it would never exist again, as they once had, before they traveled in this car. Each time they entered into sleep in this realm of man's reality, they were escorted by the signal of the Marten to seek what is required of all and to spread the experience by changing the cells within them.

The two college friends, Robert and Brandon, both went to third world countries to share what they had learned after their experience with the Astral Marten.

General Pike changed his course of action and started encouraging world peace and free knowledge, to aid in the quest to save the human consciousness.

Marcie exposed all charities to be fraudulent and disclosed how humans manipulate the poorest in society to sustain the lifestyles of the wealthy. She now helps orphaned children to find loving homes, while fully investigating the adopting family, to ensure that they meet the criteria of a model home with lots of love.

Reddick's last experience with the Marten was that he felt the car was trying to communicate with him. He could feel the sensory of nerves attempting to signal his mind. It had taken some time to unravel the layers so tightly constraining him. He discovered how his sex addiction caused him to not exist as a loving human being, due to the enormous amount of cells consuming his reality. He withdrew from the government's offer and instead reached out to his producer friends for help and guidance. Reddick is now producing films of enlightenment and the unlimited ability of the mind. His most valued piece is his own story and discovery of how he was lost in darkness, until he drove the Astral Marten. He also discovered there are no seventy-two virgins waiting in another realm for carrying out acts of darkness on others directed by the religion who uses sex to lure men into darkness. Reddick traveled in his sleep and encountered men who were trapped in a dimension that they could not get out of. They told him they were lied to about the seventy-two virgins, IT IS ALL A LIE! These men pleaded with him to help them. This was not something the Marten could help with, because these men were in a dark realm within their mind. The Marten was not created to enter these realms of Darkness. There is only one powerful spirit that could, though. Reddick knew of only one man that could help these lost men and it was the Messiah. He told the men to "Call on him to help you. He will send for your release. The Messiah is Love and only wanted to educate us all when he walked among man. The same ones who encouraged you to do the act of crime are the very ones in a past time, who also murdered him, in order to stop him from freeing us all." Reddick conveyed to these men, "He forgives you for your weakness." After this experience, Reddick's life began to change, even just moments after he awakened. He immediately recalled himself parting from the spacecraft. These men were impacted by the truth and in a nonviolent manner. It was the very experience of the Astral Marten that allowed Reddick to enter that realm to help guide all those men to slowly see the light on their own terms. The Vibration of the car broke through the multiple levels of constraints laid by society and allowed Reddick and others to eliminate the barriers in the way of their understanding, and allowed the interaction with each person's cells to occur, but in an innocent, playful way.

The Marten will never trespass anyone's free will. The Marten interacted with the higher self of each candidate to create a mission to seek total freedom and to be granted gifts of power to help others to gain the power to free themselves. It was the higher self of each person who granted the Marten the clearance to proceed with the spirit, as it is required in order to engage the spirit. Atlantis is still all about choices and free will. The darkness of individuals who were drawn to materialism and greed, intended to use the Marten to carry out their own plans to further their own cause by using this car to become more powerful in this realm of man's created illusion. They all chose to rent the car after reading about it in a science magazine and others heard by word of mouth. They used their own Free Will to engage with this alien being. These individuals were tied into darkness, and the Marten gently communicated with their higher self to gain permission to evaluate their cells. This was a huge success for the Atlanteans. This impacted the purpose of the Marten tremendously.

The ones who did not personally experience the Marten still stand a chance to be awakened. Remember the pyramid mentioned early on in this fascinating story? The pyramid really does exist in a building where it is considered to be the highest of power in the third dimension of man's reality, where most all spirits are trapped in this dimension of reality controlled by man. The pyramid idea and design originated from the highest of all realms. It was thought of in the purest and powerful realm and designed and built in this realm to aid in the protection and saving of the human consciousness. It has existed in the White House for almost eight years, now. It serves to cause the sanctioners to fall from power, because the colors represent the highest realm of all realities.

The Marten's alien energy witnessed the gold beams of light shooting across the planet in all directions. Not limited to just the United States of America, but all countries serving to gently awaken the spirit to connect to the higher self once more. The human creator of the pyramid was instructed to build the pyramid by the higher realm, specifically by the Messiah! The lady did so knowing she represented the higher realm in the pyramid with great honor and respect. The crimes against all cultures of being enslaved for various reasons. Unbeknownst to most...This Pyramid was the symbol of freedom, in honor of the most unjustly enslaved culture for the longest stretch of time known in the history of man, which is the beloved Africans. The higher realm has allowed man to place the noose around the neck on their own free will in order to save themselves from their own ignorance. The first pyramid was sent to the White House shortly after the election of the First African president. The lady who made and sent that pyramid received a response note from the White House, thanking her for her gift, so there is confirmation it was received. The full meaning of what it meant and where the idea originated from was not disclosed to them, but the presence of the pyramid in that place has awakened millions! Look around at what you see. The system is in chaos and the culprits exposed, no longer hiding under the tablecloth. The elites are being led to believe through their arrogance that being known as corrupt will aid in their mission – to continue to block the two realms from uniting. They are in for a rude awakening! This is part of the plan of the higher realm – to reclaim its spirits back to total freedom, being they were only loaned to this planet so that all could benefit from the experience of experimenting with materiality by direction of the mind. This planet was tucked away and hidden, before it was compromised by a few, who had a personal vendetta against the higher realm. The fallen spirits returned and brought with them the hijackers. It has been a very long time for us here, trapped in this false dimension. To the Atlanteans or to the highest realm, time is not measured in the same way that we measure it here, in this atmosphere of Earth, but it has felt long enough to them, so that, even to them, it seems time is dragging. Those fallen spirits were cast out, due to their infidelity with Earth women. They were supposed only to guard and watch and protect, but they almost contaminated the higher realm with the impureness of their actions. They were detected, because they informed a much younger, but loved Guardian spirit, and expressed in detail how they exploited the women with their experiences of intimacy. This guardian was not just any ordinary guardian. He had many gifts the other guardians did not know he possessed. He reported his findings to his mentors and suggested to his personal mentor to read the cells of these other spirits, because anything experienced in the human (material) realm would be recorded accurately in each being's energy field. It would be disclosed in the cells of their experience. It was then discovered that they did engage with the women of earth and that is why they were cast out and banned from existing in the higher realm, and of Earth, with Earth beings who also once existed in the higher realm. The fallen ones returned with the invaders, who successfully invaded and took over planets for their elements and to enslave the consciousnesses of the beings on those planets, including Earth. The collective human consciousness of Earth is slowly awakening, after this unfortunate ordeal that the entire world has been forced to suffer and exist under.

If the specially made pyramid is destroyed, that act will not eliminate its energy and purpose and why it was created. Because it was created by the acts of a lady who, in the previous cycle of life, was instructed by the other realm, specifically by "The Messiah," to create this powerful symbol in her next cycle. It took this lady to die in this realm and be brought back to life to break the barriers and constraints of this reality created by man. Upon her survival, this lady started to see the world much more clearly than she ever had before. The Free Will of this lady was used to design and create the pyramid, using the elements provided by this planet, in a stained glass form. Only three of these special, stained glass pyramids were created. The colors of Black, White, and Gold are so powerful in the message of what each of the colors stand for and their meaning. These colors correspond to the original three cycles of consciousness, the Bronze Age, the Silver Age, and the Golden age. The Astral Marten confirms that the pyramid is the means of the higher realm of all realities to communicate telepathically with the lost spirits trapped here, in this atmosphere called Planet Earth. The system will continue to steadily dismantle and fall apart, in order to correct itself. The corruption connected to the power and greed will soon be nonexistent, and as this transformation happens, all human beings will start seeing a change ever so slightly. To preserve everyone's free will, it has to be done in a gradual manner and by using a safe method, one that prevents and avoids the shock factor.

Many have been conditioned, beyond their current life, to exist as drones, who follow orders of a small group who decide the fate of us all. These drones will do whatever they have been programmed to do, unless they begin to examine and question what is going on. The main factor here is to learn the truth and know it well releasing the design of man from your database. Changing the paradigm will change your cells. Once the entire planet has awakened to the shift in consciousness, the turmoil you have endured during this cycle, and many from your past, will no longer exist in your memory bank within your cells. Each person will inadvertently forget it all and will not recall the hardship experienced here, in this hijacked and created reality. The cells will only record bliss, love, and forgiveness, which will act to erase the ability to recall the emotions of stress and despair. The keepers of this reality murder freely, to purposely create horrible situations that give us trauma, in order to have us all record in our cells the darkness that creates the separation of the higher self by the emotions of fear, lack, and hatred. Again, look around you, at news of riots and mass shootings, of wars, gang fights, and murders in the name of religion, how so many are killing each other, fighting over elements of the Earth, that are not really anyone's to have, hold, or keep.

This is a well planned out scheme, and they almost got away with it. But, there are those who have figured things out. These have developed the ability to see, so that the things done in secret aren't secret any more. We all must love more, give more, and forgive all of their shortcomings. Nearly all are still in the awakening process, and they, too, need patience and understanding. Some were taught in far worse circumstances than were others, depending on where they were geographically located. I only see and only accept a unified world of love and peace. We must all pitch in to save each other. By doing so, we will build an alliance of strength, sending a message to the rest, loud and clear. We know who we are, and we will not be blindsided by the illusion of death. That is a false paradigm intended to create fear. Reddick learned there is no death and there are not seventy-two virgins awarded to those who carry out acts of darkness, while committing suicide. Using sex as a reward for perpetrating acts of darkness is a huge lie created by a cult. It enslaves the mind.

The greatest act we all can do is to be steadfast in saving the human consciousness, which we can only do when we have first saved our own. We all look at our body and hold it in the highest honor of power. Please see beyond the anatomy of who we are physically, our inner spirit of energy is what is front and center, and the nourishment we provide to it will carry us into the realm of bliss. Our cells record every step we take, while we are on this path of improvement. We all must express great balance in what we have and do. We cannot save the consciousness, while being willing to kill for a pair of sneakers. We all must not be possessive to anything material, not even our partners. Possession and ownership is not love. Trust and cooperation is love. Helping each other is love. Taking whatever we can get before it's gone is not love. We must experience all we can, minus the acknowledgment of lack. Many achieve much wealth during their life. But, then it is discovered something is still missing. Many won't be able to put their finger on it, but things or possessions will never give closure. That is because it is a false paradigm. We have been taught that things are what we require. Our greatest accomplishment is to understand the science of how we create with the mind and the vibration of the elements that are waiting to be formed into your desires and thoughts. It is powerful! Money only sustains what has already been for a very long time. To me, it is not a challenge at all. Money creates dependence and prevents the mind from engaging in the science of the creation process. The cells in your body are where the proof lies. The Astral Marten will continue to save us from our enemies here on earth. Pay attention to what is going on around you. Remember the purpose for being here, which is to love, experience, and share. But most of all, forgive others who have had much worse than you have, and whose behavior reflects this lack in their lives. Look at the ones who exist in the toughest environments in other countries. Please also consider who they could have been in their previous life. A soldier instructed to fight for his country and freedom, to only be killed in that part of the world, may become, in the next life, the oppressed.

Our energy picks up and starts over near the geographical location that it last recorded in the cells. Don't be so fast to point a finger and assume that a person is not worthy of life or of rest from constantly thinking only of survival. It could be that your best friend, who did not make it out alive, as you did, is now in a brand new disguise, and you are unable to identify who they once were to you, possibly due to an age gap or culture gap. Keep your mind open, and do your best to not judge. The shift is happening, so don't miss a chance of a lifetime. The Astral Marten and the pyramid are carefully guiding all spirits back, ever so gently.

Message to the Reader From the Author

I really and truly did witness this event that played out before me, including the couple at the traffic light and the used car lot, the old house, and the reading of the letters and pictures. All these events would lead me to write this book, in honor of all Science Fiction fans. I realize it can be hard to grasp, with regard to experiencing what I did. I know the mind knows every answer to every question. We all have been trained to shut down such abilities of the mind. That purpose is to keep us all bound to this existence. It is a guarantee to the facilitators, who have the agenda to bring about an outcome that serves their purpose and not humanity's. I challenge every mind to go out on the limb and not fear the unknown. The outcome of strengthening the mind will yield to all that using the abilities of our minds is what creates all we are and what we will be. The mind can split an ATOM in half; this is fact and not fiction. I see, within my mind, you all mastering the success of this knowledge. The trick is to THINK! See the world in harmony, even in light of what is being reported. Close off the signal of chaos from your mind. Within your mind, see the experience of calmness, love, and unity. Revisit those visions often, and eventually, the vision builds up the cells of that experience, and it will become a reality. There is never a material item, nor all the money in the world, worth more than this knowledge. Our love for each other is the glue that unifies and holds the universe together.

With all my Love and Gratitude,
Melinda Pearce